THE
DARK
DECEPTION

by

JANE McCARTHY

Rae's attention was so distracted by the radio announcement of an escape from a nearby sanitarium that she almost ran over the bedraggled girl, drenched by the rain, who was waving frantically. She picked up the waif and stopped with her at a motel to spend the night, discovering when the stranger was dried out that she bore an uncanny resemblance to Rae herself. Thus began a strange succession of events marked by deceptive masquerades and mingled destinies and Rae's education in the truism that truth is not only stranger than fiction, but frequently more dangerous.

THE DARK DECEPTION

THE DARK DECEPTION

by

JANE McCARTHY

LENOX HILL PRESS

1974

THE DARK DECEPTION

CHAPTER ONE

The old blue Road Gripper took the curve
twisting grotesquely in the wet wind, which tore
laboriously, its tires singing on the pavement
that wound through the wooded terrain, afford-
ing glimpses of the sluggish gray sea below.
The girl behind the wheel did not relax her
grip, nor did she allow herself the luxury of
more than a glance at the oddly shaped cypresses
relentlessly at the car as though to protest its
unbidden entry into the deepening desolation.

Had she made a mistake, Rae Creveling asked
herself, in setting out for Colby Cove on the
vague directions of the gas station attendant
without spotting the small fishing village on
a map? It was growing darker, and if the heav-
ing motor should suddenly die—

Suppressing a shudder, she fumbled for the
unfamiliar dials on the dashboard to distract
herself and twisted the knob of the radio. The

announcer's voice wavered uncertainly, the muffled words indistinct, then cleared with a sudden volume that scratched at her nerve ends.

"—Late this afternoon when guards were distracted by a male patient armed with a knife. Doctors at Morely Institute advise that the escapee is cunningly persuasive and that extreme caution by used in apprehending—"

The remainder of the announcement was lost in the screech of protesting tires and a gasp of horrified shock as, wrestling with the wheel, Rae fought to avoid hitting a tan pick-up stalled on the hairpin curve just ahead. "Oh, good Lord—!" Her own pale reflection in the windshield, blurred in the dash lights, was all at once superimposed by the vision of a rain-drenched girl in slacks and scarf, frantically waving.

Rae braked, still trembling, and leaned across the seat to open the door.

"Hi!" She smiled tentatively and asked more seriously, "Trouble?"

The girl approached rather warily, she thought. Strange for her to be so suddenly shy after flagging Rae down. Rae noticed that the eyes, under a dark fringe of bangs, were ringed with weariness. Her face was thin, too, the flesh clinging tautly to the bones over her cheeks.

Rae imagined that the child's body was too thin under the enveloping folds of a shabby man's topcoat which hung loosely about her. While they gazed at each other in that first moment of silent appraisal, Rae thought pityingly that it was not so much her emaciation that was notable as the odd wildness in her stance. It was as if she might bolt again into the windy night if something startled her. Beyond her the headlights struck the half-toppled truck, its two right wheels mired deeply in the wet sand of the road's shoulder.

"How in the world did you manage to get in such a mess?" she asked. "Get in. I'll take you as far as I'm going." She slid across the seat under the wheel, and the other girl obeyed her, moving sinuously like a cat. Rae released the brake, and they began to move.

"Gramps always said I wasn't much of a driver," the girl said when they were under way. Rae thought, in a spasm of relief, that at least she had folks. She looked so much a part of the wilderness, a poor abandoned thing without roots or care, in her helplessness. Her next remark was surly and resentful. "They were always saying things like that." She tapped her chest lightly. "Things that made you hurt inside."

The road was even more treacherous as they climbed, and Rae had to devote every sense to manipulate the car on the short and perilous twists. She dared not imagine what lay below, what rocky chasms or tree-covered gorges. "I know," she assented bitterly. "They want us to behave like adults when we are children, and when we're grown, they insist on treating us like infants. By the way, although you didn't ask, I'm going to Colby Cove—near there, any-way—where I have lodgings for the night." The ragged tone changed to one of comfortable as-surance. "We'll have a nice hot dinner; then you can share my digs while we send someone to tow in your pick-up." When the passenger didn't respond, she added cheerfully, "Better than that, you can bunk with me tonight, and we'll send for your truck tomorrow. This rain's bound to let up before morning. O.K.?"

"Yes, that will be fine," the other agreed in-differently. "There's a side road ahead, on the right hand, where you turn to Colby Cove."

"Oh, I'm not going that far tonight," Rae said. She laughed lightly. "I want a hot bath and a long night's sleep before I present myself to Mr. Mundy—that's my new boss, and this will be my first meeting with him. Have to make a good impression, you know." She glanced at her companion briefly. "Do you know the Marine Museum? I mean, you *do* live around here, don't you? Maybe you know Mr. Mundy."

"I've been away," the girl said in a flat voice. "I've been away for a long time, and I don't know anybody any more."

Rae was conscious of a morbid curiosity. "Somehow I got the idea that you live around here; that you'd been on an errand, or something, from your home."

"No."

"You're familiar with the country, though. You knew that side road that leads to Colby Cove." She felt a rising disquiet at the contradictions. The girl had mentioned having a grandfather, and she had definitely known the road to the Cove.

The other one gave a hollow, mirthless laugh. "I used to, but I hoped I'd never see it again."

"But you were headed this way," Rae said accusingly.

"Just passing through, except that that darn car conked out on me." Her manner changed abruptly, momentarily quieting Rae's suspicions. "You're awfully good to me," she said, "and I'll take you up on bed and dinner. Thank you," she added shyly.

"Oh, that's all right."

"I guess I was lucky that it was you, a stranger. I guess my luck has taken a turn for the better."

The neon lights of the motel loomed ahead, red and blue and yellow, blurred by the mists, and Rae strained forward eagerly. "Let's hope it's good luck for both of us. I've left everything I ever knew and invested all I own in this venture," she said desperately. "It's *got* to be a fair exchange, because I can't go back. All the bridges are burned. Well, here we are!"

She left the girl in the car while she registered inside, under the scrutiny of a sleepy-eyed clerk. "How long you staying?"

"One night."

"That'll be eight bucks."

She counted out the money from the wallet in her shoulder bag. "I have a friend with me, and we'll want twin beds. When we're settled, I'd like dinner sent in."

He produced a menu from somewhere under the counter. "That'll be five bucks more. Chicken, steak or fish."

Rae ordered chicken—for some remote reason she thought it might be the safest choice—then went back to the car. Her passenger was huddled against the door, oblivious to all that had been done for her comfort. At the cottage assigned to them, she moved stolidly to help Rae with the bags from the trunk. Her mien was one of co-operation faintly tinged with abstraction. When Rae switched on the lights and they stood side by side looking at the impersonal room, Rae saw the water dripping from the girl's coat.

"The thing to do," she said practically, "is to get you out of those wet clothes." She hoisted a bag to one of the beds and opened it, tossing out a pair of tailored pajamas. "You're drenched. Take a bath first, and soak long and hot. Dinner will be here when you've finished."

The girl took the pajamas and, without removing her sodden coat, turned obediently toward the bathroom. "What is your name?" Rae called after her.

The drooping shoulders squared in momentary defense. "Celia."

Rae laughed at the ruse. "That'll do as well as anything. You can call me Rae."

She watched as Celia closed the door and heard the click of the latch. What a funny little creature! When the water was running full force and she had laid out her own nightclothes, she sank into a chair and lit a cigarette. What a crazy mixed-up day! Her muscles were cramped with weariness and her thoughts muddled. She ran her fingers through the long dark hair and stared stupidly at the table lamp, concerned only with the immediate prospects of food and rest. How long ago it seemed since her heart had been wounded—years instead of days.

Visions flashed before her eyes. Val, lithe and sun-browned in swim trunks, drawing her close to him on the dock. She could see the drops of water on his sun-bleached hair and eyelashes as his face came closer to kiss her. "Beautiful!" The low, lazy voice, the blue eyes showing crinkles of white at the corners, the mouth mutely tender. "My own beautiful girl!"

There had been that summer, sun-splashed and laced with fun and tense with the growing knowledge of what was between them. There was the swimming and the dancing, all the laughter and the quick darting from the Yacht Club to the Olympic Hotel, the late walking on streets that smelled of hot tar, the theater and supper clubs. All too swift, too fraught with sweetness to last.

The scene shifted to her apartment on a winter afternoon, with herself playing with the

drapery cord by the window and watching the
falling snow, not daring to look at him, while
the full import of his words fell on her senses
like hailstones.

"I don't understand, Val. I can't grasp it all
at once. You *knew* that she—that you and
she—?"

"It wasn't—" His voice failed miserably, and
he cleared his throat. "I'm not saying that we
hadn't talked about it, Rae, but it was just that—
talk. Like sometime, like maybe, you know?
We were kids—just crazy kids." He paused hope-
fully, and when she did not speak, he rushed
on to get it over with. "When I saw her, I
knew! Oh, Lord, how can I explain it? Something that happens like that—well, you know
it's been inside you all the time, deep inside!"
He gave a disaparaging chuckle at himself. "I'd
been so damn *stupid!* That's the first thing Beely
said to me: "You've been so damn stupid, darling!" She wanted to know why I hadn't come
after her, and I should have— Lord, on hands
and knees! She'd waited, the poor kid, waited,
eating her dear little heart out all the time while
I—"

While you were swearing eternal love for me!
Rae pressed her knuckles to her mouth to stifle

the sob in her throat. *While we were swimming and dancing and loving and kissing?*

"I guess I knew I wasn't happy," he went on fatuously, "but I didn't know why. I just kept going along and going along to dull the ache, trying to forget her, maybe—I don't know. It wasn't any good, I know that now. Just self-deception."

Self-deception! The hailstones beating against her heart were hard silver bullets now. If only he would go away! The snowflakes were smaller now, and the street below was covered with a hard cold whiteness—like death. She held herself stiff against the torture of renunciation.

He was almost jocular, relief threading through the next remark, glad that he had done the right thing and that the interview was nearly ended. "I know I can count on you to be my friend, Rae. We've had a lot of fun together, and I—well, I thought I owed it to you to tell you face to face myself. You're the first to know. That was Beely's idea, you know. 'You'll have to go to her in person,' she said. Oh, you'll never know how generous and sweet she is! 'No after-thoughts,' she said. 'No guilty conscience while I am in your arms, darling, forever.' "

Oh, bully for Beely, Rae thought on a rising

tide of hate.

"You'll meet her when we come back," he went on, "and you'll love her. Everyone does. She wants to have a get-together—Sally and Butch, Fred and Giselle—all the old gang." Rae could hear the preliminaries of his departure behind her, the gathering up of overcoat and brief case—he had come straight from the office, he said—and the slight rustling as he rose. Would he touch her? "I guess that's it, Rae. There isn't anything else to say."

"No." The word sounded like a croak. "No, there's nothing else to say, Val."

He hesitated, wanting to leave yet not knowing how to make a smooth departure. "I know it's been a shock, sort of. You'll wish me luck?"

"Good luck, Val."

He moved toward the door, not quite satisfied, and fumbled with the knob. "If there's ever anything I can do for you—?" he said tentatively.

She didn't turn. The effort was too much. If she moved, she might splinter into hard ice-cold particles before his very eyes. Just go, oh please go so that I can hold this searing agony to myself alone—all alone!

"Goodbye, Rae." Softly, compassionately. Not "darling" any more, or "my own beautiful."

Not any more. Never again the tender nuances for her alone. The latch clicked, and she held it all in, waiting for him to reappear again on the snow-shrouded street below. His collar was turned up, and snowflakes had settled on the smooth, fair, beautiful head as he signaled for a taxi.

It drew to the curb, and she saw the profile, the good-natured boyish smile, before he got into the back seat. Beely would be waiting for him, cozy before some fire, the folds of her hostess coat spread prettily about her feet, heedless of the fact that the world had caved in.

"Goodbye, Val," she called to the departing cab. "Goodbye—goodbye—*goodbye!*"

It was a scream, anguished, agonizing, tortured, suffering—and the snow fell soundlessly.

CHAPTER TWO

The bathroom door opened, and a towel-draped stranger stood in the cone of light.

"My God!"

Rae fumbled at the arms of the chair in an ineffectual attempt to rise as Celia floated toward her, an enigmatic smile tugging at the lovely curve of her lips. The sallow, too thin face was flushed and radiant from the steam and the warmth of her bath, and a cascade of dusky hair hung to her shoulders, upturned at the ends. She took Rae's hand to lift her and drew them both to the dresser mirror.

"Isn't it amazing? I noticed the likeness right off, but I knew you didn't see it."

Rae stared at their twin images, shock changing gradually to a burgeoning delight. "Who would ever believe it?" she said slowly. "With your scarf on and that coat—no, I didn't see it. It's remarkable!" She turned to view the girl more critically. "You're shorter—thinner, of course, and—"

"—and not nearly so pretty."

"Oh, yes, you are, too!" Rae assured her amiably. "But why didn't you say something back there on the road? Wasn't it a shock to you, too?"

"Not particularly," Celia said easily. "I've always felt that I had two selves—not like this, not in looks especially, but inside. The me who's like you, and that other one."

"The other one?"

"The one that everybody hates." The churlish tone had come back into her voice, and discontent marked the planes of her face. Rae was relieved at the imperative knock on the door.

"That's the man with our dinner," she said. "You'd better get into something."

The sandy-haired boy took his time transferring the food from tray to table, laying the silver carefully while his eyes darted about the room. "Two?"

"Yes, my friend's in the bathroom," Rae said, trying to hurry him along. "I'll take care of the rest. You can go now." she felt a touch of panic at the idea of his seeing her flesh-and-blood replica. "That will be all," she said, slipping a tip into his hand. "Good night."

His amber eyes slid over her admiringly, lingering. "You're sure you and—er, your friend—won't want more coffee or anything?"

"Quite sure," she said firmly, "and we won't want to be disturbed again tonight."

"I'll have to come back for the dishes," he reminded her slyly, his eyes wise.

"Leave your tray, and I'll put everything outside the door."

The chicken, cooked in a white wine and cream sauce, was delicious. They ate ravenously, buttering biscuits, anxious to fill the cavities so that they could speak once more of this miraculous attraction that had somehow melded them into one. Rae had shrugged off the tiredness and the sadness of memory in the present and awfully exciting discovery of their oneness. When she had finished, not doing the excellent meal justice in her haste, she leaned back in her chair and lit a cigarette.

"We could have been sisters, you know. My family name is Creveling—a long line of intrepid ancestors, pioneers, who came West to conquer the wilderness and distinguish themselves later in the professions along the Coast as doctors, lawyers—" She laughed to deprecate the note of pride creeping into the recital. "You name it, and there was a Creveling or a Grayson mixed into it somewhere along the line."

"No, we're not sisters or twins or cousins," Celia said. "Nothing like that. I could name those in my background, too, and they might seem impressive to some—Aunt Olivia, with her fading beauty, who was the toast of New York in 'Juliet,' Cousin Greg and his poetry which might or might not be great some day—he's abominable! There're musty portraits hanging along the balcony, mostly military men in plumed hats and gold braid—" She broke off with a sigh. "Oh, but they were not Americans, so they hardly count. No," she went on thoughtfully, "there weren't any Crevelings or Graysons. The resemblance we have is something more than that of blood."

"I don't think I understand."

"Deeper—soul."

"You mean reincarnation? Something like that?"

Celia gestured impatiently. "I don't know, or care really. When I was small I used to indulge in daydreams—imagination, they called it —and I was forever getting into trouble. They accused me of lying and said it was bad—

naughty. I was sent to the throne room—oh, never mind that!"

"The *throne* room?"

"Not really. That was more pretense. If, in those long hours, I could pretend that I was the princess about to ascend the throne—there I go again. I want to forget all of it—everything."

Rae took a long drag from her cigarette and stubbed it out. "I can't see a thing wrong with imagination. It's the beginning, the prelude, of creative thought or action, it seems to me. For instance, 'Cousin Greg'—wouldn't his poetry suffer without the stimulus of imagination, without dreams?"

"This bores me," Celia rose from the table and plopped down on the bed.

"Sorry!" Rae said stiffly. "I'll stack these dishes and go take a bath."

"I didn't mean it that way," Celia said in quick contrition. "I meant that—well, where I came from they call it 'cycling,' and, I don't know why, but the term always made me mad."

Rae frowned. "Cycling?"

Celia took the tray from her and put it outside. A gust of wet wind swept into the room, and she closed the door sharply. "Cycle and non-cycle," she sang in imitation of someone else. "If you're in-cycle, you can do almost anything you want—sculpt, paint, write—anything. Off-cycle, and you're supposed to study, practice, clean your room, put your clothes in order— just drudge."

Rae stared at her curiously, trying to estimate the difference in their ages. "This was at school?"

"The only trouble was," Celia mused, "that I was always *in*-cycle."

"Sounds like some new method of education," Rae offered vaguely. The other girl was probably still in her teens, she thought, yet surprisingly mature in some ways, and a trifle stealthy in others. She called good night over her shoulder and marched determinedly into the bathroom. Enough of this confusing double-talk for tonight.

When she came out, Celia was asleep and curled up like a kitten on her bed. Rae stood looking down on her for a long time in wonder. The petulance had given way in slumber to an innocence so vulnerable that it made her throat catch. A mere child, pathetic and pleading for something. Love? mercy? understanding? Who would want to harm her, casting her into this abnormal role of defensive suspicion and aloofness? Yet she *had* seemed sweet and friendly enough during dinner until the subject of cycling had come up. What peculiar kind of school had she been attending, where, and why had she run away?

For by now Rae was convinced that the furtive little fugitive was a runaway. It all figured—her secretive manner, her resentment and actual dislike of her relatives—her grandfather, Aunt Olivia and Cousin Greg. The girl moved, and Rae hastened to turn out the light. She must have a talk with her in the morning and persuade her to return home.

The rain had eased to a rhythmic drizzle when Rae woke to a murky dawn. Gathering her consciousness slowly, she glanced at the other bed, saw that it was empty and that the bathroom door was closed. Celia had awakened and was getting dressed in there in order not to disturb her. Moaning softly, she settled down gratefully for another little doze, a mere nap before she would have to face the day and her new life. The rain was soothing, the bed worn to the shape of her body, and she drifted off to sleep luxuriously.

When she woke again, it was with a start and

a sense of impending catastrophe. Had some sound awakened her, and where was Celia? She saw with dismay that it was after ten o'clock. "Celia?"

There was no reply from behind the closed door. Rae rattled the knob sharply, opened it and glared into the tiled emptiness indignantly. Celia must have gone to the motel coffee shop for breakfast. Her appreciation of the girl's thoughtfulness was mixed with irritation. Now she would be late for her interview with Mr. Mundy. She showered quickly, protecting her hair under a tightly wrapped towel. She had decided to wear the navy blue, severely cut and businesslike, for this important first meeting. In their initial correspondence, Mr. Mundy had objected mildly to her youth.

"Although your recommendations are excellent," he wrote, "and there is no doubt in my mind of your capabilities in this field, I anticipate that the museum board might be reluctant to employ anyone so young. In the past, marriage has terminated several of our curator contracts—"

Rae wrote firmly that she had no intention of marrying, ever, and that she was much older than her twenty-one years, having been on her own since age eighteen. Then, just in case he might bring up the matter of her health, she had a complete physical examination and sent him the results. This seemed to clinch the matter, and Mr. Mundy had written warmly, naming a date for an interview.

Putting her affairs in order, packing and subletting her apartment had occupied Rae's mind with other things than her own grief. She found in the interim that she could read of Val's and Beely's pre-nuptial parties on the society pages without going all to pieces. Still, she desperately hoped to be far from Seattle by the time their wedding took place. It would be too painful, too terribly humiliating, to face Sally, Giselle and the rest of the crowd and cope with their pity. And now she was well away from them all and ready to assume a new identity in a new life.

"Oh, dear heaven, how I need this job!" she said half aloud as she emerged from the bathroom. "I've *got* to make a good impression and, darn it, here I am—late."

Celia's old coat and boots were still on the radiator where she had spread them to dry the night before. Rae paused, frowning, to stare at them. One arm of the coat dangled limply, and there was a long smear of grease along its cuff.

The shabby loafers were still wet, and the skirt and sweater soggy. Good heavens, had the child, in her eagerness to telephone for a tow truck, gone to the office in robe and pajamas? Rae went to the closet where she had hung today's apparel. The simple dress and matching coat were free of wrinkles, the blue pumps placed neatly beneath them. Now for a clean slip and underwear.

The luggage rack was empty. Frantically she began to search—under the beds and darting from closet to bathroom in a frenzy. Gone, too, was her purse. In dawning horror, she rushed to the window to pull back the draperies.

Her car was gone!

Black despair descended like an avalanche. Celia, that sly little cat, had stolen everything she owned—car, money, credit cards and clothes. Desperately she began to dress, murmuring over and over, "Oh dear God, please—please! No, she's just gone to get a tow truck! Please let it be so!"

In her pajamas and barefoot? No, she had to face it! She's gone—she's been gone since daybreak when I first woke up—maybe before that. She must be miles from here by now. At least she had forgotten, or overlooked, the clothes in the closet. I must report this at once. Hurriedly she combed her hair, all thoughts of the interview with Mr. Mundy erased from her mind.

The night clerk had been replaced by a thin-faced woman of indeterminate age. She looked up from the papers on her desk with a perfunctory smile. "Good morning. I'm afraid you're late for breakfast."

"Look, I want to report a robbery. My car, clothes—everything has been stolen!"

"What unit are you in?"

"Number thirteen."

"The twin?"

"Yes. I picked a girl up on the road last night and—"

"A hitchhiker?" the woman exclaimed with a grimace of disapproval. "You shouldn't have done that."

"It was raining and her car was stuck. I—will you call the police for me? Maybe they can send word ahead and catch up with her."

The woman regarded her worriedly, unwilling to accept the story which would discredit her establishment. "Let me get this straight, miss. You say you picked up a girl on the road, a complete stranger, and took her into your room for the night? Why would anyone traveling alone do such a thing as that?"

"Never mind," Rae said impatiently. "Just call the police, please, and report it."

"I certainly will," the woman said grimly. "Sheriff Dalton will get to the bottom of this quick enough."

Rae watched her dial, her emotions in a turmoil, and clutched the edge of the registry while she listened to the one-sided conversation. "Picked her up on the highway—stole everything." She listened, her black eyes regarding Rae warily, her mouth compressed. "Yes—yes, that's right Sheriff." She placed her hand over the mouthpiece to ask, "Did you say your name is Miss Creveling?"

"Rae Creveling, yes."

"And the other girl?"

"She—I didn't ask. She seemed to be running away, and the only name she gave me was Celia."

The black eyes remained on her as the woman repeated this information to someone on the other end. They widened in something like fear as she protested, "Now listen— but look— the sheriff's left already? All right, I will but, for heaven's sake, I hope he hurries. I'm alone here, and I—

Rae heard a click from the other end and asked expectantly, "He's coming?"

The woman's manner was conciliatory. She backed away from the telephone and from the desk. "Now, you just sit down over there and wait, honey. They'll be here pretty soon, and everything will be fine. Just sit down over there and be a good girl, see?"

Rae refused to sit. "It seems to me that they're wasting time coming here," she declared in annoyance. "Why didn't he send someone after my car? I tell you, everything I own is in that car!"

"I know it is, honey. You sit down now, and the sheriff will take care of everything."

Somewhere in the back of Rae Creveling's mind a question prodded.

Why is she so afraid of me all at once?

CHAPTER THREE

The man behind the desk was heavy, florid and striving to be kindly.

Rae thought irrelevantly as they talked that he might have been lifted bodily from a television series, so typical was he of the half-comic Western lawman. "All I ask," she said crisply, "is the return of my belongings and my car. I do not wish to perfer charges against that poor girl. She is too pathetic."

"Pathetic—how, miss—did you say Creveling?" he asked with fresh interest.

She wanted to scream, to rend her clothes and rant at him to get on with the chase. "I don't know how," she groaned, "or why. She just *was!* —all wet and scared and obviously running away from home or school, from something. Won't you just start after her, Sheriff Dalton, or send word along the route?"

"You said you didn't know which way she went."

"I don't, no, but she was familiar with this region. She told me how to get to Colby Cove, and once she said something about hoping she'd never see this part of the country again."

"Uh-*huh*," he said noncommittally. "Odd, though, that you can't remember your own license number."

Rae shook her head in annoyance, the dark hair falling about her face. "I only bought the Road Gripper three days ago. I haven't had time to memorize it, and *she* took the license and pink slip, along with everything else. What on earth do I have to *do* to get some action?"

"Likely there'll be a mite more action than you bargained for pretty soon," he countered dryly. He waddled to the door and crooked his finger at someone. "Now let's go over that girl's description for the deputy here, so's we can see if maybe he knows her."

Rae held onto her patience with a visible effort. "Dark hair, blue eyes—rather thin and about my size. You saw the clothes she wore in my room—a man's coat, sweater and skirt, loafers and scarf. I don't think she had any money, although I didn't ask. Her name was Celia—no last name. I didn't wish to pry because she was so shy."

The sheriff raised his bushy brows to the deputy, and the latter gave a nod and asked, "Could you describe her car in more detail?"

"No, I couldn't see it very well in the rain and darkness. It was tan—I saw that much. A small truck." She broke off indignantly. "Surely you've found *her* car by now!"

"Yes'm."

"Then why on earth am I sitting here like a parrot repeating all this over and over?"

The sheriff spoke lugubriously, cutting off the tirade. "Sister, tell me, did you ever play you were someone else when you were little?"

Rae was bewildered by the change of subject. "I don't know—I suppose so. Why?"

"Just askin'."

It came to her in a thrust of recognition. She sat forward, hands clasped in relief. "Oh yes, I see it now! You've found her, haven't you? She told you that I was her 'other self,' didn't she? That we were not only look-alikes but soul-mates as well?"

Two pairs of eyes regarded her pityingly.

"We *do* look much alike," she went on eagerly. "The same hair and eyes and build. I hadn't noticed until she called my attention to the resemblance. It was so dark, and the coat and scarf—" She paused, scanning both imperturbable faces apprehensively. "Good Lord! You *do* know about the resemblance. But how? Unless," she went on talking more to herself than to them, "you know *her*. That's it! You're protecting Celia, aren't you? That's why you haven't done anything." She jumped to her feet, words jumbling together in this latest outburst of wrath. "What sort of lawmen are you? Just because I'm a newcomer, you let her get away with all my worldly goods. Now listen to me: I want a lawyer! I want a lawyer and I want justice, do you hear me? I'm sick and tired of all this sneaky subterfuge. I won't stand for it! I demand that you call Mr. Mundy at the Maritime Museum at once. He'll identify me! I was to have had an appointment with him this very morning for a job interview. Call him!"

There was a restless movement of feet before the deputy came over to push her gently into the chair again. "Take it easy, Dina. You mustn't get upset, see? Dr. Albright's coming and—" his plain homely face brightened—"he's bringin' Celia with him. That's what you want, isn't it? To see Celia?"

Rae relaxed, nodding. "Yes, of course. She'll clear this up. It's a case of mistaken identity, that's all. Last night we laughed about it—about Grandfather and Aunt Olivia, too, and Cousin— oh, what was his name? Gray? Grey—something like that. She'll see the humor of her little joke and set you folks straight. Where did you find her? At the garage?"

"We'll let her tell you all about that," the sheriff said.

Her brows drew together, and she fixed the deputy with her clear uncompromising gaze. "What did you call me just now? Dina?"

He smiled, his wide mouth listing to one side. "That's right. Pretty name, don't you think? Ever hear of Dina Boulleray?"

"No, should I have?"

"Nice little girl—pretty too," he went on sooth- ingly. "I've known Dina since she was 'bout that high." His hand measured a distance from the floor. "My old man used to work out there at The Knob 'fore he died, trainin' horses. Dina had a little pony. Rode like the wind, too, till she got bumped off on her head one day. Pony's name was Blaze—red as fire and like a streak of lightning he was. Yessir!"

"I told you I'm a stranger here," Rae said

coldly. "I'm from Seattle. There is no reason to suppose that I'd know this person." She glanced at her watch. "How much longer must I wait for Celia?"

The sheriff rose. "That's enough, Bolly. Think I hear them coming now. You sit right where you are," he said to Rae. He lumbered to the door and flung it wide. "Well, well, Mrs. Shelby!" he said heartily. "Mr. Boulleray couldn't make it? How do, Mrs. Wood. You ladies step right inside. Your little girl's waiting for you."

Rae heard a fretful voice inquire, "Aren't Dr. Albright and Celia here yet?" Then, as she emerged into the room from the hall, the woman let out a sob and came rushing toward Rae, holding out both hands in maternal entreaty. "Oh, my poor Dina," she wailed, "wandering around all night in the rain." Rae felt herself swallowed in billowing sleeves and pressed against the woman's breast. "Why did you do such a thing, you naughty precious? You've had Grandfather—all of us—worried half to death."

"Let me, Mrs. Shelby," a strong voice said as Rae struggled futilely in the embrace. Released, she looked up into a merry ruddy face. "Why, dearie," the plump little lady chortled cheerfully, "where in the world did you get that funny dress? It makes you look years older."

"It's mine," Rae said confusedly. "Who are you?"

Another sob escaped the other woman, and the little lady made a gesture of silence in her direction, saying playfully to Rae, "Now, don't you go teasing poor old Woody, dearie. Your auntie and I have come to take you downstairs to the car. Here, let me wrap your coat over your shoulders. It's a nasty day." The sheriff made a remark under his breath, and Mrs. Wood said, "They're parked down in front, and so is Mr. Boulleray. He wants to see her first to be sure she's all right."

"This gets crazier and crazier," Rae exclaimed, shrugging away from her. "I don't understand any of it." She appealed to the sheriff. "Where is Celia?"

"She's downstairs, dearie," Mrs. Wood said soothingly. "Grampa wants to see you first; then you can go with Celia."

"I don't *want* to go with Celia!" Rae's voice rose hysterically. "I only want her to return my car and my clothes. I'm fed up to here with this charade, and I'm long overdue at Colby Cove. Don't you understand?" she begged of the deputy. "I'm apt to lose my job!"

"Oh, oh, oh!" Mrs. Shelby cried. "Why aren't Dr. Albright and the nurse here? Celia could give her a shot or something."

"Mr. Boulleray doesn't want her sedated yet, Mrs. Shelby. He wants to see her first," Mrs. Wood said firmly.

Rae lunged for the door and, when the knob wouldn't turn, whirled to face them with animal ferocity, arms outspread. "What are you trying to do to me? Sheriff, why don't you stop them? I *told* you it was a case of mistaken identity. Now *why* don't you explain?" When he didn't reply, twisting his hands in embarrassment, Rae went on persuasively, "I've told them and I'll tell you, *I am not Celia!* She ran away with my car, don't you see? I came here to report the theft, and they—all of you—think I am she. Look at me!"

Mrs. Shelby raised her head from her hands and looked, then with a moan lowered her face again. Mrs. Wood said, "Celia is not mad at you any more, Dina. She just wants you back, that's all, dearie."

"Back where? At the school? She may belong there, but *I* don't! I tell you she ran away, and I picked her up in my car last night. We stayed at the Haven Motel; they can vouch for that."

Mrs. Wood lifted her brows at the sheriff, and he nodded. "That's right. We checked it out with the owner and the night clerk and the waiter who took in the supper."

"You see?" Rae jeered.

"Only thing was," the sheriff continued, "this girl was the only one in the room. Ordered supper for two, he said, but no one else was there. Ate it all herself."

"Celia was in the bathroom!"

Sheriff Dalton shook his head. "We checked it out."

Mrs. Wood demurred, "That dress isn't hers. She must have got it from somebody."

"Don't know about that. All the clothes she made her getaway in were there. Nothing else in the room, though."

"She *stole* everything else," Rae shrieked. "Now I want out of here immediately; I'm going to call Mr. Mundy and get this whole affair squared away."

"Never saw her," the sheriff said to Mrs. Wood. "Couldn't identify her if he wanted to."

"No, he's never seen me," Rae said hotly, "but he'd recognize my writing. We've been corresponding about my job here for the past several weeks. If I had my purse I could show his letters. Oh, please, all of you!"

"Hallucinations!" Mrs. Shelby seemed terriby shaken. "This will be very hard on Father. Sheriff Dalton, will you help Woody with her? We had better get this over with."

Rae struggled, clawed and called for help as they dragged her down the corridor. Heads popped out from behind doors, but no one made any attempt to help her, and when her cries were muted by the elevator, she continued to fight silently with animal ferocity. When at last they were on the street, she looked about stealthily for some means of escape. Good sense forbade her running, for they could easily catch her. She stood panting like a trapped thing, wild.

"Here's Celia, dearie," Mrs. Wood said placatingly.

A white-haired woman approached from the direction of a tan van. A nurse's cap was perched jauntily on her head, and she wore a blue cape over her uniform. Rae had a sudden impulse to laugh. There ought to be some men in white coats, she thought wildly. She twisted away from restraining hands and ran to a big black car drawn close to the curb, wrenching open the door.

"Oh, please," she panted to the man in the back seat, "take me away! Hurry! They're after me, and they think—" To her horror, she saw Mrs. Wood climb into the front seat beside the driver. "She's one of them!" She clutched at her rescuer's arm, whimpering. "Oh, sir, please let me go with you—please!"

One of the hands folded on a cane crept to her knee, patting it clumsily. "Of course you can come home with Grandfather, child—certainly!" He leaned forward to say, "You see, Woody, she *wants* to come home. Didn't I say that, if she showed any inclination, we would keep her with us?"

"Yes, sir, Mr. Boulleray," the woman faltered. "Oh, thank God, sir, thank God!"

"Have Olivia dismiss those ghouls at once!"

"Yes, *sir!*" Mrs. Wood slid out of the car with alacrity, marching importantly toward the sheriff and his deputy. Rae, huddled close to the old man, saw her gesticulating toward the car and shaking her head adamantly. So this was a friend, she thought, comforted, and the man at her side was her deliverer. She could not be grateful enough.

"Thank you," she said humbly, and sank against him trustingly. "I don't know what would have happened to me if you hadn't been sitting here. I'll explain it all before I—" She had been about to say "Before I go." But where would she go? Somehow she must get to Mr. Mundy, but for the present might it not be wiser to coast along on this welcome reprieve? She lifted her head to look at her guardian. Frail, wise and kindly, his face smiled down at her indulgently, and he drew her to him gently.

"You've never asked that before, Dina—to come home with Grandfather. If you had—ah, it might all have been so different; so very different, my dear." He laid his cheek against her hair. "And yet what might I be letting you in for? I don't know. Woody's all right," he ruminated, "a good, simple soul. And Martin up there, he's dependable at least. But, oh my dear, there are others!"

Mrs. Shelby came to the car, white-faced and angry. "Father, I fail to see your reasoning. Dina was perfectly wild in there, frightening everyone and screeching like a banshee. How do you expect *me* to handle her when it took two strong men and—"

"Get into the front, Olivia," Mr. Boulleray ordered abruptly. "Mrs. Wood and I will want Dina to ourselves."

"Ride in front with Martin like a servant? Father!"

"In front, Olivia!" Rae thought she detected a grin of triumph on his visage as she obeyed. "I don't recall asking you to manage anything. It's a relief that you've given it up." His grip tightened about Rae's shoulder. "As for this wildcat, she's tame as a pussy now."

Rae watched with relief as the nurse got into the van up ahead and it moved away. Mrs. Woods puffed to the curb and, seeing Olivia in the front seat, heaved her plump form in beside Rae.

"That," she wheezed, "took a bit of doing."

Rae peeked around at her from Mr. Boulleray's arm. "Am I supposed to be crazy?"

"Not that I ever knew of," Mrs. Wood said loyally, and Rae heard a derisive snort from the front.

Mr. Boulleray's words echoed in her ears: *"But, oh, my dear, there are others!"*

CHAPTER FOUR

Boulleray's Knob defied description, situated as it was on a high rocky bluff. Rae's first impression was that the stony fortress had grown from the gray crags surroundings it on three sides. In some places the mountain had broken apart into cruel crevices, down which rain rushed in a roaring waterfall. In the lesser holes and caves cypresses grew, twisted and gnarled by sea winds. The scene was all the more dramatic because it had been approached through a flat wooded lane of elms and maples. In that first moment of panic Rae thought that her protector had deceived her and that this was a place of incarceration.

His next words reassured her. "Home, Deeno! Remember how I used to call you Deeno?"

Rae wanted very much to please him, not only for his own sake, but also to hide her repugnance at the ugly, monstrous house looming before them. "I remember." She smiled.

He was scrutinizing her face, feature by feature, with clear blue eyes under bushy white brows. "You've grown very beautiful during these years, my dear—the formative years, I believe they call them. You are quite a young lady."

"Still packed with mischief, I'll wager," Mrs. Woods said fondly. "Do you recall what you used to call your grandfather when you wanted to wheedle something out of him?"

Now they were both watching her expectantly —even suspiciously, Rae guessed. Why? Did they, perhaps, need assurance that her mind was normal? For the more she considered the matter, the more certain she was that the girl of the night before had been mentally unbalanced. This accounted, she reasoned, for Celia's quick changes of mood, her rudeness in some instances, and the final caper of sneaking away with all that she needed to lose herself completely. Rae felt a stab of pity for the confused child. Could she get by with it?

They were still waiting for her reply, so she hazarded a guess. "It was something silly, I know. Gampy? Was that it?"

They both chuckled, and Mrs. Wood said, "That's close all right. Gimpy."

"That was after I hurt my leg," Mr. Boulleray said. So that accounted for the cane, Rae surmised. She shuddered to think of the pitfalls which lay ahead before she could make her escape and seek asylum and verification from Mr. Mundy.

Olivia, spoke, interrupting the reminiscences. "Disrespectful, if you ask me. Undisciplined. I shudder to think of Greg's behaving that way to his grandfather."

Aha, Rae thought, Cousin Greg enters the picture. What was it that Celia had said about him? That he wrote poetry and that he was "abominable." A divided household under the authority of an aging crippled patriarch, and poor little Celia the pawn. Playful, teasing, unpredictable, Celia had been coddled and scolded by turns until—until she had lost her mind? Oh no, she wasn't that badly off! Something else rose to her memory: the deputy saying, "She fell off the pony and bumped her head." Good heavens, hadn't it occurred to these people that Celia might have suffered a severe concussion which had affected her memory and nervous system?

The big black car slid smoothly to the portico, and Martin went around the front of it to assist Mr. Boulleray to the veranda, slowly and very carefully. Mrs. Wood gathered up gloves and her bag, chirping, "Oh dear, don't tell me I left my parasol in that nasty police station—"

Rae rescued it from the floor. "Here it is, Mrs. Wood."

" 'Mrs. Wood,' " the lady repeated. "My goodness, you *are* grown up, dearie."

Rae felt the need to correct herself. "Woody?" she said tentatively.

"That's better. Hop out, dearie, and let's see about lunch. Cook will be furious."

Martin was back at the car again, waiting impassively, and Rae was astonished at his clean good looks and his youth. From the back, his broad shoulders had given the impression of maturity, but now she saw that he could not be more than twenty-five, might be even less. Aware of her scrutiny, the chauffeur let one eyelid drop significantly in an otherwise expressionless face. Rae stifled a giggle. I'm going to like you, she thought impulsively.

Mrs. Shelby, murmuring complaints, was already inside, and Rae could hear her calling, "Greg, Mother's home, darling, and we have a surprise. Father, you're not going upstairs?"

Mr. Boulleray was handing his coat and hat to a stiff-necked, balding man. "No, Olivia, I am not," he said with feigned patience. "I am having luncheon with my granddaughter so recently restored to me. Come here, my dear," he said to Rae.

Rae saw a dull flush rise to Olivia's rather piquant face. "Very well, do as you please, but I warn you, you're overdoing it, Father."

What had Celia said about her? That she was a fading beauty who had once played "Juliet" to New York audiences. Yes, from the way she moved with practiced grace and the throbbing tones of her voice—Rae could imagine the past triumphs. If only she didn't complain so much and so peevishly, she would still be lovely. Soft fair hair, possibly helped along artificially, warm brown eyes—Rae wanted to like her, meant to do so. Olivia had been very affectionate at their first contact, she remembered, until Woody had taken over with her more practical approach.

"Look familiar?"

Mr. Boulleray was regarding her expectantly again. She looked about the mammoth hall, mentally recording the stairs, the umbrella stand, the ferns and benches, and responded brightly, "It all looks so wonderful! I—is anything changed at all?"

"*I* am." She turned to see a youth leaning nonchalantly against the newel post. "I am very much changed, Cousin Dina, since you whipped my mare with a hickory stick, then lassoed us both with your rope." His eyes, dark like his mother's—for this *must* be Greg—glinted with malice. "I'd be equal to the situation now."

Rae was impressed with his fair good looks, with his expensively casual clothes and his superior demeanor. He looked as though he had been put together with a practiced hand and displayed with devotion. The hand on the newel post was slender and long-fingered, the hand of a poet or an artist. She groped in her mind for an appropriate reply. "And so, let us hope, have I, Greg," she conceded agreeably. "I promise never to be so rude again."

Instead of being mollified by her overture of friendship, he retorted through tight lips, "As if you'd get the chance, you little fiend! I've always hated you, you know."

Olivia moved to defend him, slipping her arm through his and whispering, while her eyes lingered on her father's face in trepidation. However, the old man seemed disinclined to make an issue of the matter. His fingers on her elbow urged Rae toward the dining room where, at the end, a small table had been set for four.

Wine glowed in crystal goblets on snowy damask, and silver sparkled. Rae, accustomed to TV dinners at a breakfast bar in her tiny kitchen, caught her breath. "For me?"

"Mrs. Wood probably telephoned ahead," Mr. Boulleray said. "Very thoughtful. It looks nice and festive, Woody."

"Thank you, sir."

"Right down to the fatted calf," Greg said, holding his mother's chair. "If I had gone away to the loony-bin and returned a prodigal, it would have been peanut butter on stale bread in the kitchen."

"Gregory!" his mother implored.

"That's about enough, Greg," his grandfather warned.

The boy gave a hollow laugh. "Call it an 'institute of learning,' if you wish—pretend, if it assuages your guilt. Morely's Institute is a nuthouse, nothing more or less, as Dina can no doubt verify." He sat down and shook out his napkin. "Tell us, Dina, how was it? Did you acquire the fine veneer of sanity, the thin façade of respectability behind those grim walls?"

Rae didn't know what to say. A reproving murmur passed around the table. "I felt fine," she said with some heat, "until a few moments ago."

"Touché!" Greg said in sardonic delight. "It's going to be a pleasure to have you about to spar with."

"That's enough!" Mr. Boulleray said angrily. "Olivia, either persuade your son to behave himself or tell him to leave the table."

Greg helped himself to a generous portion of steak and kidney pie with insolent insouciance and, although he said nothing more during the meal, Rae could feel his malevolent glance on her from time to time. She wondered if, should she behave herself very well, she might subdue his animosity and win his mother's trust for "Celia's" sake. Surely the child would be found eventually and exposed when her fragile mask of forgery and theft was torn away. And when she was and the entire plot was exposed, Rae resolved to deal gently with all of them—the ones who liked her and the ones who did not.

The meal progressed more quietly until, from somewhere above, a deep basso split the silence with a rich rumbling passage from "Hawaiian

Wedding Song." Rae listened, enthralled. The others went on with their lunch. The sound broke off, and Olivia said, "I thought Pick was to stay at the winery this month."

Mr. Boulleray replied with placid amusement, "Perhaps he divined by some occult source that Dina was coming home." His eyes danced mischeivously as he turned to Rae. "You have no objection to seeing Pick, have you? Pick Nichols?"

"The tree worshipper?" Greg taunted. "The big guy who was so smitten with you?"

"I'm sure you must be exaggerating," Rae said mildly, hoping the remark would suffice.

"I should think he'd remain where he was sent," Olivia snapped.

The traps were growing numerous, Rae thought. Now she was to be faced with someone who was smitten with her. What was she supposed to say and do? She listened apprehensively to footsteps coming down the stairs, accompanied by whistling. Mrs. Wood came in from the kitchen just as a huge apparition of a man appeared from the hall. His chest was enormous, the rest of his body slim and lithe, as is so often the case, and he was meticulously clean, combed and groomed. His smile was wide and innocently cordial as he glanced around the table, then suddenly fleeting as his gaze rested unbelievingly on Rae.

"Dina!"

The deep voice made the name a musical chord.

"Hello—Pick," she managed to say. "How are you?"

Silence had fallen on the little group in deference to this reunion; all of the faces were rapt with attention. The big man's skin flushed to a dull red, and his hands clenched and unclenched.

"Quite a surprise, eh, Pick?" Mrs. Wood said. "Doesn't she look fine?"

"Yeah, fine," he repeated as if in a trance.

"You've had your lunch, Pick?" the little lady asked solicitously.

"Yes, Mrs. Wood, thanks. Quite a while ago." He seemed to be recovering. "Well, Dina!"

Rae couldn't think of anything more to say. She thought of commenting on the weather, "All this rain!" or "You look the same, Pick!" but perhaps he didn't. "How are things at the winery?"—would that do?

Mr. Boulleray solved the problem for her. "If you'll help me up, Pick, I'd like to see you for a few moments in my study."

"Yes sir." It took a while to steady the older man on his feet, to get his cane and see the arthritic hand close over it just so, all of which the big man did with gentle single-mindedness. "All right, sir?"

"Fine, thanks. Dina, Mrs. Wood will get you settled, and after I've had my nap, we'll get in a game of cribbage before the fire, eh? Good day for cribbage."

"Yes, a very good day—" She didn't know whether to call him Grandfather or the pet name Gimpy. "If I've forgotten, you may have to teach me all over again," she said.

When they left the room, Greg said, dabbing at his mouth with his napkin, "Ver-ry touching."

"Pick's bashful," Mrs. Wood declared. "For all his preaching in front of thousands of people, he's just a bashful boy. Remember, Dina, how he used to *sing* the Bible?" Mrs. Wood folded her hands over her clean white apron and raised her eyes heavenward. "Never a dry eye in the house when that young fellow chants the Holy Scriptures."

"Excuse me," Greg said caustically. "Mother, would you like to come along and fill me in on the morning's trauma?"

"Greg!"

"Oh, never mind, then, if you'd rather not, Dina, see you tonight at dinner."

Olivia gave a grimace of a smile and followed her son. Rae heard them arguing as they climbed the stairs and caught a shred of complaint from Olivia, "—And you promised me—" And Greg's answer, "How in the name of thunder did I know you were bringing her here?"

"Do you want more coffee, dearie, or shall we be getting along?" Mrs. Wood asked. "I fixed up your rooms myself while you were all having lunch—a nice fire and all—and we'll have a cozy chat. All right?"

"Yes, Woody, that will be nice. I'm a little tired, I guess."

" 'Course you are! All that fuss in the village, who wouldn't be? That Celia! I could have whapped her over the head with my parasol! Such language! Some nurse!"

Rae's suite was grander than anything she had ever had in all her life. She dared not betray her unfamiliarity by looking too much, or exclaiming, but she thanked her friend for the fire in the little white and blue parlor, let her hand rest lovingly on a striped satin loveseat and sank into a low chair while Mrs. Wood bustled about, closing windows and bringing a robe and slippers from the bedroom closet.

"You cozy up in that," she said, unzipping the navy dress, "and have a nice nap. I'll come up later to run your bath and lay out something more becoming. Personally, I don't care for you in dark clothes at all."

"Mrs. Wood—" Rae reached out a hand to detain her—"you know that what I said at the station is the truth, don't you?"

The abrupt question stopped the older woman cold. For a long moment she stood, head bowed, her back to Rae, before she said quietly, "Whatever's bothering you, dearie, I'm sure it will be all right. We'd best let things be for now."

Now what did that mean? Rae asked herself when she was alone. *Does she know I'm an imposter, or doesn't she?*

CHAPTER FIVE

Rae saw Martin before he saw her. He had on white coveralls and was washing the big car just outside the garages. His hair was plastered down on his forehead from the exertion, and a dead cigarette dangled from his mouth.

"It's a Lincoln, isn't it?" she said to cushion the shock of her approach.

"Lincoln Continental—hi!"

"Hi! It looks new."

He straightened, moving his back muscles cautiously, and threw the cigarette into the bushes. "Made to order," he said, slapping a palm down on the hood. "A great piece of work." Rae noticed that there were no servile "ma'ams" or "misses" in his conversation. "How you doing up there?" he asked with a nod toward the house. "That kid giving you any trouble?"

"Greg?" Rae laughed ruefully. "He doesn't

upset me as much as he'd like."

"Good! Nice morning, isn't it?"

The cold March rains had at last given way to a sweet sunny April, and the day was magic with the smell of dewy apple blossoms and the sound of birdsong. Rae had suffered the first few days in an agony of indecision. She had consoled herself with the fact that she *had* tried to confess that day at the station and had been frustrated at every turn. Now, if she enjoyed the safety and hospitality until the rains stopped, who could blame her? During the long hours of the night she pondered on how to go about exposing her pose and apologize. Then, as the days passed and Mr. Boulleray and Woody lavished her with affection, while Olivia and Greg began to accept her as a member of the family, although not exactly a welcome one, she had settled down to a contented marking of time. After all, the job at the Maritime Museum was gone now, she was without means, and for the moment there was no other course. In Dina's rooms, comfortable and pampered, and in Dina's coats and dresses, she was beginning to feel like Dina. No longer did she hesitate when she was called by Dina's name. Often, running down the stairs in response to Mr. Boulleray's summons, she would call happily, "Coming, Grandfather!" with a real sense of belonging. There would be the usual prelude to dinner, cribbage, chess or checkers, and the two of them alone in his cozy study, sometimes talkative, often silent as they pored over the game.

"You skunked me, Grandfather!" she might cry in defeat. "I hate all that counting. I was never any good at figures."

"You're a poor loser, Deeno. How about another game?"

"With the play-off after dinner?" Rae loved these hours alone with him, when the intimate affection between them was a tangible thing. How could Celia (or Dina) ever have left him when he loved her so?

In many ways she found herself coming actually to dislike the real Dina. Evidences of cruelty, masked under the guise of mischief, kept coming to Rae's notice in stories of the past. She realized that the other Dina and Greg had been competitive in childhood and that she had used her petty little triumphs as a threat to his masculinity. She had turned his boyish confidences into weapons of ridicule, quoting his cherished rhymes from the pinnacle of her superior years and gnawing away at his talent. Greg had mentioned these insidious little assaults numerous times with lively resentment. Rae felt sorry for the bitter boy and tried, gently and reasonably, to bridge the breach of those childhood years.

"We were only kids, Greg. I'm sorry I was such a hellion."

"Was? I don't know what you're up to, Dina, slathering the Old Man and catering to everyone. But I warn you, I don't trust you now any more than I ever did."

Occasionally, too, there were questions which brought her up short, allusions to former friendships and acquaintances, or oblique references to pets and incidents pertaining to them. Sometimes she managed to counter these references with questions of her own.

"How old was I when old Daisy died?" she might ask. "I've forgotten."

"Forgotten?" Olivia might scoff. "After the way you blamed poor Greg for the accident and lied about him and shut yourself up in your room for days? Oh, Dina, for shame!'

"I'm sorry!" It was becoming a litany of repentance, Rae thought uneasily as her knowledge of Celia's thoughtless lack of consideration grew. She often wondered how Mr. Boulleray could have loved his granddaughter so blindly and spoiled her so outrageously. No wonder Olivia disliked her.

During these days of adjustment to the household and her tenuous position within it, she had one major victory which seemed to impress all of them in her favor. They were talking at dinner of some of the riding horses in the meadows, of Greg's mount, Pegasus, in particular, and Rae remarked idly on the qualities of the pony, Blaze.

Recalling the deputy's remarks about this splendid animal, she said, "he was a fireball, red as the setting sun and swift as the wind."

Pick, who was dining with them that night, said quickly, "Don't think about it, Dina."

Mr. Boulleray raised his hand. "Wait a moment, Pick. Go on, Deeno, and tell us what you remember."

What else had the deputy said while reciting his little allegory, one which was supposed to bring an admission of her Boulleray identity? "I remember," she said with a harsh little laugh, "that he threw me, the devil, and caused me to hit my head on a rock."

Pick and Greg were staring at her strangely and with a dawning respect, or was it hope?

"I don't know why we have to talk about that," Olivia fretted. "If Dina had a blackout about that evil day, she's better off than the rest of us."

"She hasn't got a black-out," Pick said shortly. "Go on, Dina. What else do you remember?"

"Well-ll," she hedged, "what do you want to know? There was an old man, a horse trainer —I believe his son is the sheriff's deputy now and—"

"So you knew Bolly Bagley all the time!" her grandfather chortled, mutely asking the others to join him in admiration. "How does that strike you folks, eh? All the time my girl was in that station, she was having her fun baiting old Bolly."

"What an actress!" Pick applauded with a deep laugh. "Olivia, she takes after you."

Olivia smiled at her softly, warmth transforming her face into a special beauty. "Dina, you amaze me—really! I had no idea that your—er— pretenses were talent." Tears filled her beautiful eyes, and she rose to come around the table and gather Rae's hands in hers. "Oh, my dear, if I had only known! I'm so sorry about all the times I scolded you for what I thought was lying."

"Aunt Olivia, don't give it another thought," Rae said generously. "I'm sure it must have been upsetting to have me 'pretending' all over the place." She recalled Dina's account of the "two selves' who lived within her. "I suppose I wanted to be exactly like you." Although she couldn't see for the life of her why they were all so pleased, Rae was delighted by their pleasure. "Oh, I love all of you!" she said impulsively, smiling at each face in turn. Greg lowered his eyes without speaking, his expression enigmatical.

That particular night when she was getting ready for bed, still stimulated by their approval of her, she asked Woody, "Why were they all so surprised that I remembered Blaze tonight?"

Woody paused, smoothing the folded counterpane in her hands. "Don't you know, dearie?"

"No, I don't."

"Well, that was the start of your trouble, that nasty accident, and that little devil, Greg, did it all, too. No matter how much his mother covers up for him, this is one thing she's never suspected: that he caused you to have your—er—breakdown. Mind you, I'd not have known the truth myself except that old Mr. Bagley saw it all."

Rae's curiosity was mounting. "The stable-master?"

"The same." Woody's lips were compressed with ire. "That no-good son of his was in on it, too—him and Greg together." Rae waited, wondering, for the rest of the story. "Blaze was fast, true, but he was gentle as a kitten with you and the prettiest pony in the corral. "That's why Greg envied you so, dearie."

"And I was selfish with my pretty pony?"

"That's as may be. He was yours, don't forget; your grandfather bought him for *you*. Specially bred and specially trained he was, all for you. Greg couldn't stand that, the little imp, and anyone could see he wanted that pony—bad. Sometimes I wonder that he can look you in the face after what he did to you—ruined your life, so to speak."

"Oh—now!" Rae protested.

"It's true as you're sitting there, dearie, and not a mite of repentance in his black heart all these years. 'I'm glad she's gone,' he said many a time. 'I only wish I had Blaze.' He rode over the hills for weeks, looking for that poor pony that he'd abused; that poor little pony tearing all over with those awful thistles under the saddle tormenting him—him that never had so much as a cross word from you. My thought is that he dashed himself to death on those black rocks up there—like a suicide."

Rae covered her face with her hands in shivering horror. "Oh, how terrible!"

Woody patted her shoulder sympathetically. "You'd no way of knowing," she said, "and I shouldn't have brought it up but, I declare, I get so riled when I think that everything that's happened was that brat's fault. Your skull split open the way it was—oh, your poor grandfather! —and then all those wasted years." Her voice changed from a note of bitter acrimony to one of cheerful optimism. "But there now! You're home and well again, and never a sweeter child lived. All the goodness and kindness in you has brought Himself up from his bed of grief and given joy to his years, like it says in the Bible. Oh, I knew the minute I saw you in that dirty office that you belonged home with us."

"But I behaved so badly that day."

"Who wouldn't? Caged up like an animal in that asylum—nobody would want to go back there after having once escaped. Now no more of this, dearie, or you'll be having bad dreams again."

"Is that why your room is next to mine—

because of the dreams?"

"Hush now. Have your bath and, as Pickeral says, 'May angels surround your bed through the night.' "

"Pick says that? He sounds like a good man."

Woody spun about to glare at her suspiciously. "You ought to *know* that he's good," she lashed out reprovingly. "Of all the people in this house, *you* have reason to know. Coming to see you the way he did, moving heaven and earth to get you out of that hell-hole—surely you appreciate that, Dina."

This was a new avenue of information, one which Rae was too tired to explore tonight. "Yes, I do," she said meekly.

When she was in bed going over the day's events, she wondered how Pick had managed to visit her in that "hell-hole" and what he had done to effect her release. Pick was the X factor, the person Dina had not mentioned. He was the mysterious quotient, and although he was kind to her grandfather, and apparently respected by the other members of the household, she didn't know quite how to categorize him. Greg had said that Pick was "smitten" with her, yet she failed to see any evidence of this in his presence. His shyness and blushing she attributed to a certain clumsiness in one his size. And hadn't someone said that he was a preacher? What, then, was his position here?

She could readily define the duties of the others. Mrs. Wood could be considered, loosely, the housekeeper; Martin the chauffeur; and Grimes she thought of as Mr. Boulleray's male nurse and a sometime butler. There was Cook, too, whom she seldom saw, and a neighborhood girl of all work, Letty, who came in on call to help with window-washing and seasonal cleaning. Olivia had mentioned that Pick resided part time at the winery. Possibly he was the estate manager.

She turned out the light and settled down for sleep, ridiculing herself for all these curious conjectures. Until a month ago she had never heard of any of these people or seen them, but now she felt as though her whole life had been moving toward this time and place, like a river flowing to the sea. Another marvel was her love for old Mr. Boulleray, which seemed to have been born in that first instant of trust when she had pleaded with him in the car for his protection and which had grown, during her sojourn here, to overwhelming proportions. Even Woody had come in for her share of affection; as for

Olivia and Greg, she felt a tolerant amusement.

Only Pickeral Nichols remained outside the pale of her emotions.

Recalling what little she had known of her own father, Rae could attribute much of the love she had for Mr. Boulleray to that parental coldness. Her mother had explained the indifference sadly in terms of disappointment. "Donald so hoped for a boy, dear, and we waited so long; then—" She had shrugged impotently. "That's why we named you Rae. His father's name was Ray."

Rae had felt deprived during her childhood when her classmates' fathers had made a fuss over them. Cool, remote, distracted, Mr. Creveling gave more of his time and affection to his students in the Seattle boys' school than to her. He always seemed to regard her, when she appeared on his horizon, vaguely and with surprise—this foundling to whom he was obligated unwillingly. He died of pneumonia after a prolonged spell of flu when Rae was eight. Afterward her mother languished in grief for ten years before she, too, let go of the strands of life. Thinking of them now, Rae admitted sorrowfully that her own loss had been minimal. She hadn't known love or how to give it, until she met Val.

Now even Val seemed like a myth. Life at Boulleray Knob had almost obliterated his features, and she couldn't believe that she had suffered so agonizingly over his careless perfidy.

She fell asleep to the sound of the waterfall tumbling down from the crags outside her windows.

CHAPTER SIX

It was not until some weeks later that she realized Martin had had a motive in asking her whether Greg was giving her trouble.

Rae was chatting with him, lingering in the morning sun after her walk, when Greg passed by on his way to the barns to saddle his horse. He glanced their way, and as Martin laughed at some remark of Rae's, stopped abruptly. "Aren't you getting a little out of your class?" he asked her maliciously.

Rae was speechless. She liked Martin and enjoyed their light repartee and always, if she saw him, detoured by way of the garages to exchange a few words with him. She admired his clean good looks, his humor and the way a cowlick on his forehead forced a lock of hair down on his brow. He had been under one of the smaller cars on his back, tinkering with some part of the mechanism, when she approached today, and had remained there while they exchanged pleasantries.

Now he stuck his head out to grin up at Greg. "What's eating you, fella?"

"I don't approve of my cousin consorting with a dirty grease-monkey," Greg retorted belligerently, glaring down on the supine form from his superior advantage. "I don't want you speaking to her again."

Rae's anger mounted by degrees. "It's none of your affair, Greg, what I do. How dare you dictate to me?"

"Isn't this getting a bit thick," he sneered. "You and him?"

Martin began to climb out from under the vehicle. "Listen here, Shelby—'

He had barely opened his mouth when Greg's riding boot struck him full in the face. Rae saw a spurt of blood and screamed. Aiming another swift kick, Greg caught him under the jaw in a thud that made Martin's bones rattle. Rae began beating the boy with her fists, teeth clenched in fury, backing him away until Martin could recover an upright position. At that moment Olivia, a flower basket over her arm, emerged from the sun room and saw them.

"Dina!" she shrieked. "What on earth are you doing? Help, someone; She's gone crazy again." She ran forward to hurl herself between her son and his assailant. "My God," she wailed, her arms around Greg, "this will kill Father! Greg, run inside and telephone Dr. Albright at once. Oh, how dreadful!"

Martin was out now and, seeing Greg's retreating figure, addressed himself to the distressed mother. "It wasn't her fault, Mrs. Shelby. Greg kicked me while I was down."

Olivia gazed, horrified, at the blood running down his chin and began to cry. "Then you— you must have deserved it. Dina, you get into the house at once!"

"I will not!"

"All right then; I'll have to get Pick to subdue you." She went off around the house with that peculiar grace, her head bowed.

They watched her silently until she disappeared. Martin dabbed at the blood on his face and felt his jaw gingerly. "Trouble! So help me, the next time I run across that kid, I'll flatten him!" He gazed at Rae contemplatively. "I'm afraid this spoils your playhouse, Dina. The Shelbys will do all they can to get you cooped up again."

"I'm not afraid," Rae said staunchly. "Grandfather will defend me. He knows I'm not mentally unstable."

Despite the gloomy prospects, Martin permitted himself an exultant snort. "The way you waded into Shelby, I almost thought you'd gone berserk myself."

"It was so unfair!"

"You want fairness? Then you'd better put on your prettiest, primmest pose for the doctor. He'll come a-running with a strait-jacket when he gets that summons."

"That's got to be a gross exaggeration, Martin!" she snapped defensively. "I have nothing to fear from the truth. Can't I do something for your face?"

He turned aside, saying curtly, "Not now—here comes your keeper."

Rae whirled to see Pick walking slowly toward her over the lawn. His eyes followed Martin's retreat, then scanned her face seriously. "What caused the ruckus?"

While Rae recited the details indignantly, he guided her back to the house unobtrusively. When she had finished, he said, "You should have called me."

"Olivia said that you would 'subdue' me. I

don't like the term, Pick, and I don't like your manipulating me this way." She jerked her elbow from his grasp. "I'm going inside, alone, to tell my grandfather about this."

"I wouldn't do that, honey," he warned implacably. "It might be fatal to him—his heart, you know. Let's figure this out for ourselves. The first thing is for you to get ready for Dr. Albright. Fix up real nice and just be yourself. And," he warned, "don't start fighting with Greg again. Right now, they're holding all the big cards."

"I just *told* you what happened!"

"And I believe every word of it, Dina. But this old game will have to be played with finesse. I'll be with you, don't worry."

Woody had said that this big bashful man had tried to get her out of Morely's Institute—"moved heaven and earth" to do so. Had she underestimated him? Yet, in spite of all his efforts, hadn't the real Dina languished in that place for several years? She lifted her chin determinedly. "I won't leave here! This is my home, and I've done nothing wrong or crazy."

Pick smiled down at her sadly. "Aren't you forgetting something—the basic facts, maybe? You may not be demented now, no, but you were

—for many years. It will take time to prove yourself anew, to the family *and* to Dr. Albright." At Rae's shocked expression, he continued, "You, Dina, as you are now, physically resemble that little girl of years gone by, but there the resemblance ends."

Does he know? Rae thought excitedly. *Why hasn't he exposed me by now if he knows?* "Do you think I should leave?" she asked.

"This is not the time to go into that. Suffice it to say that your better self has triumphed. Didn't I predict that? I've seen you give them all something almost like happiness—even the fiends are nearly human. We're wasting time. Go inside and change while I wait for the doctor."

Another friend! Rae stripped off her shirt and blue jeans and hopped into the shower exultantly. Pick! She said his name tremulously but with confidence. He was big and powerful, and he would not let any harm come to her. Let the vultures do their worst; with Pick on her side, she had nothing to worry about!

She chose a pleated white miniskirt from Dina's closet and wondered if the other girl was enjoying her clothes as much, wherever she was. A loose light blue sweater and a white scarf to tie back her hair. Pale lipstick—demure was

the note! Her own blue pumps with the tracery
of white. Pick was down there waiting for her,
and he would not desert her. She tidied up the
bath and bedroom, gave her nails a quick inspec-
tion and flew downstairs again.

Her grandfather called from his study, "That
you, girl? Have you seen Pick?"

"I— he's busy just now, Grandfather. Could
I take him a message?" She peeked around the
door, smiling at him.

Papers were spread out on the desk, and the
door of the safe hung open. "Good morning," he
said with the note of gladness he reserved for
her. "There's no particular rush but, yes, ask
him to come in here when he's free."

She promised and took her leave quickly.
Pick was standing on the front veranda, talking
to a man Rae judged to be the doctor. She went
out to them.

"Hello, Dina," the man said pleasantly. He
wasn't at all the ogre she had pictured him
to be. His hair was tan, his eyes tawny and
crinkled at the corners, as though he laughed
a lot. He wore a lightweight business suit and
had no sign of the medic about him at all.

"Good morning, Doctor," she responded, taking a chance. "Won't you sit down?" She risked

a sweeping glance at Pick and had the satisfaction of having him wink at her encouragingly. "Would anyone like coffee?"

"I'll get it," Pick said quickly. "Back in a minute."

Dr. Albright sat down in a wicker chair, and Rae took one opposite. Bees buzzed in the honeysuckle espaliered along the stone pillars, and from a distance a jay squawked his discontent. Rae folded her hands in her lap and waited for him to speak. He regarded her critically without seeming to do so.

"You look very well—very happy, Dina."

She smiled engagingly. "I am, thank you, Doctor—both." She couldn't help liking him and his easy manner. *Watch out,* she thought, *this is only a preliminary to snapping the trap shut!* "It's nice to see you."

He grinned widely, his eyes crinkling. "All right, I'll buy that if you say so. Dina, I'm going to ask you a few questions. Do you mind?"

She laughed. "Would it matter, Doctor? Shoot!"

"What have you been up to?"

"You want me to say that I had a fight with my cousin."

"Your aunt was very perturbed."

"She perturbs rather easily, Doctor, where her son is concerned. *He's* the one you should be interviewing."

"Yes, Mr. Nichols briefed me on the particulars. How do you feel about your cousin, Dina?"

"I try to keep an open mind. Greg's pretentious, sometimes arrogant, and this morning he was insolent and mean. I got mad, that's all."

His next question startled her. "Are you still in love with the chauffeur?"

She could feel a flush rising to her face from her neck. "Good heavens—" She had started to say, "I hardly know him!" and amended it quickly to, "How silly!"

"With Mr. Nichols?" he persisted. "Now that you're of age and—"

Her blush held, and she knew he saw it. "Must I be in love, Doctor, with anyone?"

He laughed, easily and pleasantly, and Pick came out with a coffee tray. Rae busied herself pouring, handling the first cup to Dr. Albright and another to Pick. When she had sipped her own, she addressed Pick.

"Dr. Albright is on a romantic tangent this morning," she told him. "It must be the spring in the air." Still smiling, she asked the doctor impudently, "Are *you* in love?"

Pick started visibly. Had she said something wrong? Dr. Albright was occupied with cream and sugar. "My wife would be interested in hearing the answer to that," he parried.

His wife? Lord, was she supposed to know her? Tension seemed to have risen in the last several minutes. "Wouldn't she, though?" Rae said lightly. "I read an article recently—I've been reading quite a lot. The rain, you know—"

The doctor leaned forward with interest. "You have? What, Dina, have you been reading?"

Rae thought of her erstwhile companion, restless and variable in her moods. *She* wouldn't have the patience to read, would she? "Oh, just snatches of things," she said flippantly, "in the magazines Woody brings me. I like the fashion mags best."

He relaxed, disappointed. "Do you still criticize your cousin's poetry?"

The other girl had said, "Greg's poetry might, or might not be, great." Rae hesitated a fraction of a second before she said, "Not lately. He might be good, though. I've never been sure, one way or the other."

The men began to talk of other things, Pick steering the doctor's attention away from Rae with the subject of grapes and the effect too much rain might have on the wine. He spoke of "the cool belt" and the "dry, sunny areas" while Rae felt a rush of gratitude. She refilled their cups, fascinated but wary. What would be the final ploy, and how would she measure up? The doctor gave her a clue which she could not afford to let slip by.

"Estelle and I thoroughly enjoyed the Chardonnay you sent us. It's fine wine."

"We're not the greatest vintners in the country." Pick said modestly, "but we're gaining ground."

"I hope Estelle is well," she said.

The doctor's eyes widened in surprise. "She'll be pleased that you asked about her, Dina. Sometime when I'm coming this way, I'll bring her along with me."

That, thought Rae smugly, *was a master stroke of genius, and he doesn't realize that he handed it to me on a silver platter!*

The doctor rose, ending the interview. "Perhaps I should speak to Mrs. Shelby before I go."

"Sure," Pick agreed. "Just follow me, Doc."

Albright took Rae's hand. "Dina," he said, "I wish all my patients were as happy as you seem to be."

"You don't think that getting angry is fatal?"
she teased.

"Not under the circumstances, no."

"I'm forgiven?"

"Completely absolved."

They smiled at each other amiably before he
released her hand and went inside with Pick.
While Rae gathered up the coffee things, she
could hear Olivia's mellow voice rising and falling in disagreement. "I tell you, Doctor, Greg
was only trying to be friendly. Then when this
fellow said something derogatory about Dina—
well, what would any gentleman do under the
circumstances? Martin will have to be dismissed at once."

"I'd like to see your son, Mrs. Shelby."

"You don't believe me?' she asked in her
best Sarah Bernhardt diction.

"And I'll wish to see Martin," he said firmly.

"I suppose Dina told you a pack of lies. You
know her well enough not to give credence to
her allegations, Doctor. I had hoped—thought—
that you'd bring Celia along and take the girl
back to Morely for observation."

Rae took the tray to the kitchen, thanked
Cook and, making sure that no one was about,
streaked toward the garages to inform Martin of

the expected interview.

Dr. Albright, although pleasant and placid, was also clever, and it would be better for Martin to be prepared for the questioning rather than surprised. In this case, she thought, his bruised face and lacerated mouth would be sufficient testimony to convince the doctor of Greg's malice and guilt.

The half-light inside the garage made vague shadows of the cars, and she called his name. There was no reply, and she was about to climb the stairs to his lair above when she heard a low moan from outside. Startled, she had the notion that Greg had hurt Martin's head more seriously than she had first perceived. Martin was in the little car he had been servicing, his head lolling against the steering wheel in a grotesque position and blood pouring into his eyes.

Rae stifled a scream and jerked open the door. "Martin! Oh, what has happened?"

His inert form rolled from the car and lay prone on the pavement at her feet, a bloody wrench beside it!

CHAPTER SEVEN

Again, Rae sat alone in the sheriff's office of the Glendale courthouse, waiting.

Every detail of the squalid room as she had last seen it was impressed on her memory—the fly-specked narrow windows, the spittoon in a corner, the scarred and battered desk and the acrid odors of stale smoke and disinfectant.

The wall clock ticked on with maddening precision, and she wondered where Woody was being detained, whether she was with Greg in some other part of this complex, or alone. Olivia would be with her son—that was certain. She would be protesting his innocence with every convincing actress' weapon at her command.

They had been a sorry, silent little group coming into town with Dr. Albright under the wheel. Greg assumed a nonchalance which was contradicted by his nervous chain-smoking, and

Woody, as usual, sat close to Rae with her bright button eyes blazing in anger. She had insisted on coming, had even appealed passionately to Mr. Boulleray for permission after Pick had set off with the victim to the nearest hospital at the county seat.

The door opened, and Rae looked up with relief, seeing not the sheriff, as she had expected, but Bolly Bagley. Relief gave way to trepidation at his first words. "Well, young lady, are you ready to give *your* version of the story?"

"Not until I have someone with me," she answered steadfastly.

His large beefy face reddened. "Oh, sure, he said sarcastically. "They always start hollering for a lawyer when they're guilty."

"In this instance, I'll settle for Dr. Albright or Mrs. Wood."

"They're both busy."

"Then I refuse to be interrogated."

His voice was rife with insinuation. "Don't have much use for the law, do you, Dina? Like to do what you want without any curbs, don't you? Seems from what I've heard so far, like you got a delayed reaction to that Martin's insults and went back to have it out with him."

Dina compressed her lips and gazed determinedly at the dirty window. This wretch before her had been branded by Woody as a mischief-maker, a pony-torturer and in league with Greg in the other Dina's accident. She heard the scratch of a match and smelled the foul stench of his cheap cigar. "You forget," he resumed mockingly, "that I knew you way back when— know quite a bit about you since then, in fact. Always kinda liked to make things tough on folks, didn't you? Well, this is one spot you're not likely to get out of so easy." He blew his smoke past her nose, and Rae rose to go to the window. She struggled to raise it without success, and he made no move to help her. "Care to start talking?"

Rae gave up on the window and turned to face him. "Not to you, no."

"Might be a long wait then."

"So I've got time on my hands."

"Might be you could get *time* another way, Dina. Ever think of that, huh? A man's been damn near killed—might be already dead, far's I know—and you're the last person to see him. What did he say to you, Dina?" he wheedled. "You must've been mighty mad after you sweet-talked the doctor—*mighty* mad."

Rae smoothed the pleats of the white skirt,

mutely refusing to cooperate.

" 'Most everybody remembers that temper of yours," he said with a snide laugh. "*I* sure got cause to remember it. I still got a scar up in my hair to remind me. It was only a piece of driftwood that time. This time it was a wrench."

So the real Dina had clobbered him in the remote past. Good for her!

"Greg, now, was always a nice little kid, making up poetry and all. Kind of a gentle boy, wouldn't you say? Never had half the stuff you had—toys and the like. Never blew up or anything like that. Never hurt anybody. If Greg was to get blamed for something he didn't do, you'd like that, wouldn't you, Dina?"

"I *saw* Greg kick Martin in the face while he was under the car helpless!" she blurted spontaneously.

"Only because that guy insulted you."

"Martin did no such thing! He's a gentleman."

"Another thing that makes me think you're a liar," he went on imperturbably, "was that cock-and-bull story about some other gal stealing your car and stuff the night of your escape from Morely's." His nasty grin widened as he imitated a popular television commercial. "It's not nice to fool Mother Nature."

"I suppose you investigated," she said acidly. "Or was it too much trouble for one of your mentality?"

"Now see here how you turn on me," he whined resentfully. "Is that nice? I'm only trying to befriend you, Dina, and the Lord knows you sure do need friends right now. If I was in your predicament, I'd act a whole lot different."

"And let you railroad me to the booby-hatch? I'll see you you-know-where first, Bagley!"

"Temper, temper!" he chided triumphantly, glad to have annoyed her. He tried another tack. "Kinda sweet on that Martin, maybe?"

Rae heard footsteps outside and refrained with difficulty from denial. Pick stuck his head inside and, seeing her, grinned widely. "So this is where you are? Come on; we're going home."

"Says who?" the deputy countered belligerently.

"Says your boss, fella." He took Rae's arm. "Martin's regained consciousness," he told her, "and he refuses to prefer charges. Come along."

They left Deputy Bagley sputtering.

"I brought my car," Pick said when they were outside. "Figured you wouldn't want to see much of Greg right now."

Rae stopped dead still on the steps, arms akimbo. "Do you mean to tell me that he denied everything?"

"I wasn't there, honey," Pick reminded her mildly, "but I guess he did."

"But Dr. Albright knows better. At least he knows where I was and that Greg was missing during the interim."

"Well, the word came through that Martin doesn't want any of us implicated. So that settles the matter—for the present, at least."

"Don't you understand? I *wanted* to tell my story—to someone responsible, of course, not that despicable Bagley."

"I hope you didn't harass him. He's mean, Bolly is."

"You're telling *me!*"

"All right, don't get steamed up all over again. I thought we might make a little occasion of this—have lunch somewhere and do whatever it is girls like to do on a visit to town—maybe buy something."

An inspiration began to dawn in Rae's distraught mind. In view of this new development, she needed help, and there was only one person who could give it to her by identifying her—Val. Perhaps she might have a chance to call him long distance from the restaurant or a nearby telephone booth. Married or not, he was her last and only chance, and with Bagley breathing down her neck, she needed to clarify her position. It hurt her to have to betray Mr. Boulleray, but with everyone else against her, this was the only course. She turned to Pick slyly, hating herself for her deception. "I haven't any money," she murmured, "for shopping."

He was pleased with what he understood to be acquiescence to his plan. "I'll take care of that and wait in the car while you buy out the town. First, though, let's eat."

The tacky little café was filled with a noonday crowd of farmers, town girls from offices and stores, and a group of Mexican fruit pickers. Pick led her to a booth at the back and pushed aside dirty cups and overflowing ash trays. "They'll thin out soon," he said, sensing her aversion.

Rae jumped as the juke box, encouraged by a teen-ager's dime, bellowed out, "I've Got A Tiger By The Tai-il." "I'm just nervous from the interrogation," she apologized. "But I warn you, it hasn't affected my appetite."

"Good!"

"What will Woody and Grandfather think about our not returning to The Knob for lunch?"

"I cleared it with Mrs. Wood. She'll tell the Old Man."

Free! Rae felt a tremor of excitement. This was the first time in almost two months that she had been on her own, and even now she must have a guardian. She made herself charming to Pick until the meal came. It was delicious, and she ate every bite, down to the last shred of meat loaf and mashed potatoes covered with glistened brown gravy. Pick finished and lit a cigarette, watching her indulgently. "Want more coffee?"

"No, I want to get on with that shopping. Do you realize how long it's been since I've been in a store?"

"Want me to tag along?"

She tapped his arm playfully. "And spoil it all? You'd just be in the way, Pick, and bored stiff. Besides, I'm going to scour the town for those unmentionables that girls love."

His face flushed as he groped in his wallet and laid some bills out. "That enough?"

"Plenty, but would you mind giving me some loose change, too?"

"All I've got," he said, complying. "The car's parked in front of the courthouse. I'll wait for you there."

"You are a dear!"

She tried not to walk away from him too fast. Where would be the best place to call from? Obviously the telephone office. In her eagerness to get it done, she inquired as to the direction from the first man she met.

"You're headed straight for it, Sister. Say, ain't you—?"

"No, I'm not," she said quickly, and left him scratching his head and staring after her. Shrinking a little inside, she realized that every resident of Glendale must know about Dina Boulleray and the tragedy surrounding her. Was that why Pick had wanted to come with her—to protect her from the natives' curiosity? Suppose he was trailing her? She must get this over with as soon as possible.

In the reception room of the telephone office, she stepped into one of a row of booths, inserted a coin and gave Val's Seattle number to the operator. Thank heaven she remembered it! While she waited, a faint humming of the wires in her ears, she wondered if he might have moved since his marriage. Besides, what would he be doing at home at this hour? She didn't know his office number. She bit her lips as a faraway phone began to ring.

"Hemphill residence—hello," an unknown voice said. They had a maid?

"Hello. May I speak to Mr. Hemphill, please? This is long distance calling."

"Long distance? Jus' a minute, please." A hand went over the mouthpiece, blurring the voices at the other end. Then another's voice, low and modulated. "Hello, this is Mrs. Hemphill. Who is calling, please? Mr. Hemphill has gone to his office."

Rae made her voice nasal. "May I have that number, please?"

"He won't have arrived there yet. May I take a message?"

Rae saw a shadow pass the outside door and imagined that it was Pick. How could she explain her presence in the hot phone booth? Nervously, her words blending and all formality forgotten, she said, "Listen to me! This is Rae Craveling, a friend of Val's, and I need help—desperately. Please tell him this: I'm at Boulleray Knob— B-o-u-l-l-e-r-a-y—fifteen or twenty miles south of Glendale—G-l-e-n-d-a-l-e—and I'm being detained here against my will. I need him to come here and identify me, do you hear? As soon as possible. I won't get another chance to call, so please tell him it's an emergency, will you?

Emergency! Hello, can you hear me?"

There was a long silence before the other voice said icily, "Really! Don't you old flames ever give up?" The crash of her receiver severed the connection.

Rae stood staring at the instrument dully. *Damn!* she thought viciously. *Talk about jealous wives! That snippy Beely!*

She went to the doors, took a quick look up and down the street, and returned to the booth with renewed decision.

"Did you complete your call?" the operator asked.

"Yes, I did. Now I wish to place another. Can you get me Mr. Val Hemphill in the Anderson Building in Seattle? He is with the Havens Brokerage Firm."

"I'll try, ma'am."

There followed a tiresome session with Seattle Information, while Rae felt beads of perspiration forming on her face and body.

"I can give you a Havens Realty on Primrose Lane."

"*No*, Operator, no! I want Havens *Brokerage*—in the Anderson Building. Person-to-person to Mr. Val Hemphill."

"Just a moment, please."

Moments were hours, and every passing pedestrian on the street was Pick! Presently the operator came back on the line and said, "We have Havens Brokerage for you now. Please deposit eight-five cents for three minutes." Her voice lifted and she said, "Mr. Val Hemphill, please. Glendale calling."

"Mr. Hemphill isn't here," an indifferent voice said.

"Where may we reach him, please?"

"Why, at home, I suppose. He no longer works here."

"May I have that number?"

Rae cut in, thoroughly defeated, "Never mind, Operator." She hung up the receiver and leaned against the booth, panting as though she had been running. What was the use? Even supposing she found Val, his wife was alerted now and would never allow him to come. She lingered on the hard little seat for some time before she rose and headed into the bright brackish sunshine. There was nothing she could do—nothing!

All her earlier exuberance deflated, she walked along blindly, impervious to the stares of passersby. Somehow Fate had relegated her to this time, this place and this crazy predicament. What if she went to Mr. Boulleray and confessed the masquerade? She would be hurting him incalculably, and besides, where could she go if she left Boulleray Knob? Exactly nowhere.

She passed a small specialty shop and reminded herself that she ought to have packages when she returned to the car. Panty hose or a slip? Maybe a present for Woody. *I could take a bus and be far away from here by night.* With Pick's money.

A gift? The salesgirl suggested a soft cashmere sweater for an older woman. The blue, or this pink with embroidered roses? "How about something for yourself? We have a new stock of darling summer dresses."

"No, thank you."

"A sun hat? Look at these stunning colors."

"Well, all right—the red one, I think. And something for an elderly man," she added as an afterthought. "That silk ascot. He wears them sometimes with his smoking jacket."

It was all a dream—a horrible, mocking dream from which she would never awaken. It was a nightmare of dark deception from which she could never escape!

CHAPTER EIGHT

"Want to drive over to the county seat to see Martin?" Pick asked some days later. "I have business with our wine distributor over there."

"Will they let me see him?" she asked eagerly.

"Sure. He's sitting up in bed now and lonesome."

After she had changed clothes, Rae went out into the garden and picked a bounteous bouquet of roses, snapdragons and sweet damp lilies-of-the-valley. This was a rare treat, and she had a sense of adventure as she anticipated the outing. Her exalted place in the household had shrunk to a new and frigid low since Martin's almost fatal "accident." Neither Greg nor his mother deigned to speak to her now, carrying on private conversations with each other during meals, while she conversed only with Mr. Boulleray, who was not notably loquacious these days.

Rae thought his health had deteriorated rather noticeably recently, and she attributed this to worry over the mysterious attack. Although they didn't discuss the matter openly, she thought, too, that his own affectionate manner toward her had cooled. Hurt and puzzled by this change, Rae wondered if, by some word or gesture, she might have exposed herself as a *poseuse*. Not only did she regret this, but it made her feel unwelcome in the big house she had begun to think of as home. This sense of disapproval made her all the more delighted at the prospect of seeing Martin. At least *he* didn't have any pre-conceived notions about her, one way or the other.

Once in the sickroom, however, she found herself unaccountably timid and ill at ease with the patient. It seemed to her that there was something regal about him in the white turban of bandages, and although his blue eyes shone with welcome, there was an entrancing aloof-ness about him. She had brought him ice sher-bert and busied herself arranging the flowers in vases and bowls while he ate. After the initial greetings, she didn't know what to say to him.

Martin was the one to break the embarrass-ing silence. "Stop fooling with those flowers,

Dina, and come over here where I can look at you."

"I'm sure I look a mess," she said, moving toward him. "I haven't slept since I found you that awful day."

"So you found me."

"Yes. I went out to tell you that Dr. Albright was going to ask you for some verification of the nasty incident with Greg. I looked in the garage and saw you weren't there, and I was on my way back to the house when I noticed you all crumbled up over the wheel. When I opened the car door, you fell out—"

"Where was Pick?" he asked unexpectedly.

"I don't know," she confessed in bewilderment. "Somewhere inside, I suppose. Why?"

"Had he been with you?"

"Yes, for a while. He was there while Dr. Albright was talking to me, except when he went to get us coffee."

"How long was that?"

"Fifteen minutes—maybe twenty. What are you getting at, Martin? More to the point, who hit you with the wrench?"

"I don't know. After I'd gone up to clean off the blood, I came back down to test the engine. Whoever it was caught me from behind—must've been hiding in the back seat. He gave me a powerful wallop, and I went down—and out."

"What makes you think it was Pick and not Greg?"

"I told you I don't know who it was," he said irritably. "Do you have any idea?"

Rae's forehead wrinkled in thought. Neither Pick nor Greg had been in sight while Olivia and the doctor were talking. Yet they both might have been there. She tried to reconstruct her own interview with Dr. Albright, paying special attention to the time element. "No, not for sure," she said slowly. "I assumed all along that it was Greg—after that unprovoked attack on you, I was convinced it was. Why would Pick do such a thing?"

"That's the prize question."

"Oh, it couldn't have been. He brought you to the hospital."

"That may have been to make it look good. It would be the best way to deflect suspicion from himself—good Samaritan and all that. They questioned you?"

"Well, yes and no. Dr. Albright knew, of course, that it must be reported to the sheriff, and it was his suggestion that we do that personally. He drove us into town—Olivia and Greg and me. Then Woody insisted on going, too. You know how she is when she decides to do a certain thing. At the courthouse they separated us, or at least me, and Deputy Bagley was assigned to me. I don't trust him and I wouldn't answer his questions—not without witnesses. Then Pick came and said that you refused to name your assailant and—well, that was the end of it." She stared down at the hands twisting in her lap and asked, "You did dismiss charges, didn't you?"

"When I came to and remembered what had happened, yes, I did. What was the use of accusing anyone without knowing?"

"But the investigation might have turned up something. Everyone but Olivia thought it was Greg getting even—having the last triumph, so to speak."

"I couldn't take the chance of having *you* implicated."

"You think I was hiding something because I wouldn't tell my story to the deputy? I wouldn't do that, Martin, and I *didn't* strike you."

"I know, I know," he said irritably, "and that wasn't why I refused to make charges. It's just that you are vulnerable, Dina. You've been confined until recently in a mental institution.

That starts you off on the wrong foot right away, see? Any one of them, with the exception of your grandfather, would be delighted to have you sent back there, for good."

Rae's eyes widened. "You're including Pick? Why, Martin, he's been the soul of kindness to me."

"Don't let that deceive you," he said harshly. "All that stands between Pick and eventual control of Boulleray Knob is you. *You,* Dina! I mean it. For that matter, he's pretty well in control of everything now—the wineries, the cattle business—everything! He had it made until you showed on the scene."

"I can't believe it of him! Not that he would deliberately throw suspicion on me. No, it's just not true! He stood by all the time Dr. Albright was there—protecting and encouraging me. And the other day in town, he took me to lunch and gave me money to go shopping—"

"You were alone in town with him?"

"I was alone with him coming here today. No, Martin, he's my friend, not my enemy. Mrs. Wood told me about how he tried to have me released from that place—how often he visited me."

Martin's eyes narrowed. "Mrs. Wood *told* you?

Wouldn't you have remembered without having to be told? *Do* you remember, Dina?"

She saw her mistake. "I was on sedatives," she said lamely, "and tranqs. Things were fuzzy at times."

"And you don't remember Pick ever visiting you?" Without waiting for a reply, he hurled another question at her. "What do you know about Dr. Albright?"

"Why, nothing, actually. He seemed nice— capable. I understand that he gives several days each week to the patients at the sanitarium without remuneration. That would indicate a splendid sense of charity, don't you think?"

He shook his turbaned head in commiseration for her gullibility. "Dina, Dina, what's to become of you?" he moaned. "After being railroaded into that place, after all that you've been through, you still think that anyone who's 'nice' to you is above reproach."

"It's just that I don't understand your antipathy toward Pick. Everyone else loves him— Grandfather, Woody. Even Greg and Olivia seem to respect him. After all, he's a minister."

"Oh yes," he agreed sarcastically. "Holy Pick spouts the gospel and sings hymns in his powerful basso—a rabble-rousing evangelist catering to the fears and superstitions of ignorant people, hypnotizing them with his big voice and big body until they are blobs of protoplasm yelling 'Amen' on cue."

"You sound bitterly anti-religious."

"Do I? That's because I've been to a few of his rallies."

"Mrs. Wood thinks they are wonderful."

"Mrs. Wood is prejudiced in his favor. Most people are. He's got a silky manner and a homely folksiness which inspires confidence. Who's to say that he might not wish me incapacitated out of jealousy?"

Rae pointed a finger to herself. "Because of me? Then why would he bring me here to visit you?"

"That beats me. Same reason, I suppose, that he brought me to the hospital—a grandiose gesture to win plaudits for good old Pickeral."

"I don't know about you, Martin. You raise doubts, but you have no answers. You can't *know* that Pick struck you. As for being jealous of our little chats, he has never shown an indication of anything but a kindly interest in me—a kind of pity, really." Her face colored faintly as she recalled that Dr. Albright had asked about her feelings, not only toward Pick, but also toward Martin. "I'm sure you're wrong about Pick," she murmured.

Martin saw the flush and attributed it to an attraction to Pick. "All right, I give up!" He sighed heavily. "Do me just one favor, a very simple one. Don't come over here with him again—not alone. Don't go *anywhere* alone with him."

Rae measured him seriously. Pale, bandaged, helpless and torn with suspicion, he was someone she wanted to humor. But she was not, could not be afraid of Pick. "That means that I'll be house-bound," she said sadly.

"Is that so bad? You've been cage-bound for a long time. And I'll be back at The Knob before long. I can drive you wherever you want to go."

"I'll be glad when you're able to come home," she said. "Woody has been making plans for your recuperation. You know that supply room off the kitchen? She's had Cook and Grimes and Letty scrubbing and painting for days. We brought down some furniture from the attic— Pick did that!—and I'm to be your nurse."

"You really mean that? You'll be glad to have me back? Why?"

"Well, for one thing, I like you," she admitted, flushing. "For another, my stock seems to have gone down pretty low. You see, Olivia and Greg cling to the certainty that I, in one of my 'wild tempers,' hit you."

"Yeah, they would," he said grimly. "What about your grandfather?"

"I'm afraid they've influenced him, too." She was on the verge of tears. "He seems distracted and sort of wistful, as though he is disappointed in me."

"That would be Pick's dirty work."

"You insist on coming back to that!" Her tone was filled with impatience. "I wish you wouldn't be so one-track-minded!"

Riding home through the evening mists, though, she found herself regarding Pick Nichols with something less than her former confidence. She wanted to analyze his most casual comment and read hidden meanings into his inquiries about the state of Martin's health.

"Does his memory seem all right after that bash on the head?"

What did he mean by that? "Oh, quite."

"No lapse of memory? Was he able to recall anything of the attack?"

"We didn't discuss that, Pick. I didn't want to distress him," she lied.

"I see. What did you talk about?"

"Mostly about his coming home."

"Yes, he's probably anxious to get out of there. Martin's an outdoor type."

It sounded to Rae like a criticism. "No one likes to be cooped up," she said rather defensively, and added deceptively, "I least of all."

He took his hand from the wheel and dropped it warmly over hers. "You know that we were doing everything, Mrs. Wood and I."

"Then how was it, Pick, that you were so surprised to see me that first day at lunch?"

"Was I surprised? Perhaps I was, yes. You see, I'd been living at the winery during the busy time, and to come home and find you sitting there—"

"My grandfather made the decision, and that's all there was to it. Isn't it strange, though, that he thought I didn't *want* to return to The Knob?"

Pick, she thought, looked disconcerted. "You —I know you weren't quite yourself, honey— but you alienated all of them—all of us. For instance, that story you told about someone stealing your car and belongings—Celia, was it? That kind of thing isn't calculated to make you popular."

Rae tried to pout as she had seen the real Dina do. "I didn't like her."

"You like Dr. Albright, don't you?"

"I guess I have mixed emotions about him. Sometimes yes, sometimes no.

"You've got to trust *someone*, honey."

"I've been accused of being *too* trustful."

"Martin said that?" he asked quickly, suspiciously. "What else has he been telling you?"

Rae saw her mistake and again took refuge in the real Dina's subterfuge. "I don't want to talk about it any more. I'm tired."

His lips were compressed and his brow wrinkled with thought for the rest of the trip. When the lights of the house penetrated the fog, she got out of the car without speaking and went to her room. There she stood with hands clenched, listening to the waterfall rushing over the rocks—down, down, down—to some hidden deadly abyss.

I must leave here, she thought desperately. *Somehow I must get away from this farcical masquerade!*

CHAPTER NINE

In the weeks that followed, Rae came to the conclusion that Pickeral Nichols emerged from every dilemma unscathed, admired and applauded. He was the one who finished the painting in Martin's room, working painstakingly and winning praise for his artistry from everyone.

"I had no idea of the extent of your talents and capabilities, son," Mr. Boulleray said fondly. It had been a long time since he had spoken thus to Rae, and she felt a twinge of envy of Pick. During all these days she had been berating herself mercilessly for fostering a blatant deception. It had gone far enough, she scolded herself, and she must be on her way before tragedy struck again. Although she still felt Greg to be the guilty one, she observed Pick ever more closely. And she asked herself why

Martin would assume that the foreman would be the eventual heir to The Knob holdings in the event of Mr. Boulleray's demise. Wouldn't Greg, his grandson, be the logical choice? Or Dina?

Martin's homecoming proved to be anticlimactic. Although his room was shining clean and decorated with spicy autumn chrysanthemums, he showed no appreciation after he had limped from the car. He shrugged off Pick's helping hand, passed Rae with only a glance, and sprawled on the bed in agitation. He was angry! Perhaps he had accused Pick of the dastardly deed and they'd had an argument.

Rae asumed her duties anxiously. She brought him lunch and hovered over him while he ate. She offered him the new magazines Olivia had brought from town, carrying on a sprightly conversation about anything and everything. His head had been shaved, and he kept running his hands over its bristly surface.

"No, I don't want to read, I don't want to talk or play silly games," he lashed out. "I'd like to be alone."

"With pleasure," she said disparagingly. "You're a lousy patient. My mother used to say when my father was sick that this is a good sign of recovery. An obnoxious patient—" She stopped, realizing that she had nearly exposed her own personal background. Apparently Martin didn't notice. He turned his face to the wall in mute dismissal.

Left to herself and filled wtih disappointment in the reunion she had looked forward to for so long, Rae wandered through the house like a lost soul. Greg was out riding, and Olivia had driven off after lunch to one of her committee meetings. Upstairs, Woody was supervising Letty in a drastic fall cleaning. Rae could hear the scrape of furniture being moved and saw Grimes climbing a tall ladder to remove the screens and install storm windows. As always, there was the sound of running water from the falls behind the house, a dismal noise on this dismal day. She called to Grimes, asking that he leave the screens on her own windows, then went to the library for a book she had been reading. She had been delving into the letters of Keats and thought, with him, "Oh, for a life of sensations rather than of thoughts!"

The book was gone, and she ventured into Mr. Boulleray's den to look for it. The room was dim in the half-light of the cloudy afternoon, and she was almost to the desk when she heard the rustle of the big leather chair where Mr. Boulleray usually sat. The high back concealed his figure, and she called apologetically, "Sorry to disturb you, Grandfather. I think I left my book in here."

The chair swiveled around, and she saw that it was Pick. He held in his big hands a scrap of paper which he quickly thrust into his jacket pocket. "Oh, it's you, Dina. Come in, come in! What are you reading?"

She handed him the book which had been lying open, face down, on one of the chairs. "Keats."

He turned it over and perused a few lines. "You'd do better to be getting acquainted with the Bible," he boomed in his rich voice. " 'O ye of little faith—' "

"Why do you presume that I'm not familiar with the Bible?"

"Because I know you, Dina—or used to." He held out his hands, fingers splayed. "Like the palm of my hand."

"Don't you imagine that every person has secret places of the heart and mind, protected places where no one else is allowed to intrude?"

"Secrets are dangerous," he countered sanctimoniously. "The prophets counsel us to be open and aboveboard with our fellow men—"

Rae headed off the homily with a little laugh. "Maybe I'm becoming a nature-worshipper, reading this and *Arcadia.*"

"You're not the same person you once were," he said wistfully. She had never noticed before the full heaviness of his lower lip. Now it hung protrudingly in an over-size pout.

"I take that to mean that you recognize me as sane," she quipped.

"Not quite. I take you to be the victim of your own emotions, Dina."

"Oh?" She took up her book, resolved to escape this verbal summation of her character. "You could be right—"

"Always striving, struggling—"

"Excuse me, Pick. I must look in on my patient."

"That's another thing—what's between you and Martin?"

She thought this over before she replied, "Mutual consideration, maybe. That ought to please you, Pick, with all your admonitions to consider our fellow men."

"No, I'm not pleased. Not at all. There is something intrinsically evil in his power to influence you."

"You're saying that Martin is evil?"

"The devil is very real and very powerful, and he assumes many guises to deceive the innocent."

She gave him a twisted smile. "Once you accused me of not having enough trust. Shouldn't I trust Martin? What happened between you and him on the trip from the hospital, Pick?"

His eyes narrowed, and he rose to pace the floor with cat-like tread. "So he told you that, did he? That we disagreed? It's true. He has contempt for my work with souls—satanic contempt."

"Well—" she shrugged facetiously—"what's a little contempt when you have so much approval?"

He reached her in two long strides and took her shoulders in his strong hands, shaking her roughly. "Don't you see why I'm sorry you're here, why I opposed it? You are too vulnerable to suggestion. Oh yes, you're smooth and poised on the outside, but I know, Dina, what poison roils inside you—what rottenness! You're like a beautiful flower, one that's deadly to the touch! I've tried to help you—I want to help you—but you retreat into your own private hell. I can see it in your eyes when I try to save you." He clutched her to him in a frenzy of protectiveness. "Oh, Dina, why won't you be mine—mine alone?"

Confused and bewildered by this sudden change of mood, Rae released herself from his hold. "You're hurting me, Pick! I'm trying to like you, to understand the things you say, but you seem so queer."

"I've done it all for you—everything! I love you, honey—I've always loved you. You know that! Do you think I'd let Greg, or Martin either, jeopardize all that I've built up for us? You're so stand-offish with me, so cool and aloof since you came back." His forehead was wet with sweat, and Rae backed away from him, repelled. "That day at lunch—for a while I thought you were the old Dina, simple and uncomplicated, depending on me, believing me."

"Did she—the other Dina—ever tell you that she loved you?" she asked bluntly, her eyes wide on his damp face.

"Honey, what are you saying? You were just a kid. I told you I'd wait for you to grow up. I was working all the time toward that, and you knew it."

"Pick, I *am* grown up now," she said solemnly, "and I don't love you—not like that. I'm sure I never did."

His face, gleaming with perspiration, turned purple in the diminishing light. "It's that Martin!" he said through clenched teeth. "Oh, don't think I haven't seen you waiting for him, laughing with him, letting him change you! I had to stop it!"

She flung the accusation in his face, her voice shrill with discovery. "So you tried to split his skull with a wrench! You tried to kill him! Is that what your religion recommends—murder?"

"Justice!" he thundered. "Justice and judgment!"

Rae backed toward the closed double doors, thoroughly frightened now by the fury on his face and the glazed eyes glaring at her balefully. Her hand was groping for the knob when it turned and the door was pushed against her.

"Oh, Dina—Pick!" Mr. Boulleray blinked at them in the dim light. "I wasn't aware that—"

A complete transformation came over Pick. His face paled, his voice resumed its normal tone, and he turned on a table lamp. "I was trying to find that paper we spoke of, sir, and Dina came in for her book." His intent look dismissed Rae. "She was just going back to her patient."

"And how is Martin?" Mr. Boulleray asked,

sinking into his chair. "Does he find rooming in the house to his liking?"

"Yes, I think so," Rae stammered. "He'll require lots of rest for a while."

"And you'll see that he gets it? Take good care of that boy, eh? He's quite a person in his own right, to say nothing of his illustrious ancestry."

Rae's heart leapt. "His ancestry?"

"But then you know about that."

Pick glared at her from behind the old man's chair, and she said, "Yes, of course. I keep forgetting that Martin was ever anything but a chauffeur." She clutched the volume to her closely and, almost whispering, said, "I must go."

Everything had come to a standstill, and the very air vibrated with mystery. In these last few minutes, Pick had almost admitted that he had struck Martin with intent to kill. He had admitted other things, too—that he was protecting Dina's rights, assuming that he would share them with her. And—another thought struck her cruelly: He had *opposed* her release from the institution! Hadn't Woody said that he had tried to *obtain* her release? Was this another of his poses? She felt chilled at the brutality of his revelations that afternoon.

Martin was awake and seemed refreshed by his nap. Rae made coffee in the deserted kitchen and carried the tray into his room. He had risen from the bed and was seated weakly in a chair.

"Are you ready for coffee and company?" she asked lightly to test his mood.

"Your company, yes," he said, stressing the pronoun. "I'm sorry I was so beastly to you earlier. What's the news around here, if any?"

She busied herself with cream and sugar, handing him his cup as she asked, "Martin, how long have you known me?"

"Just about forever." He grinned. "What is this—an inquisition?"

"Did you ever believe me to be mentally unstable—insane?"

He sobered and set his cup aside. "Never! I was with you at least a part of every day when we were kids, you'll remember, until I went to Vietnam. When I came home I was shocked—horrified is a better word!—to hear that you had been at Morely's for nearly two years. I came at once to see Mr. Boulleray, and we had a long talk. I could see that he shared my doubts about the necessity for such a preposterous procedure, although at first he tried to justify the action by saying you'd been incorrigible. Then he said, 'The sad thing is that she doesn't want to come home.' "

"That's what he said to me that day in the car."

"You were in a bad state that day."

"Yes, I was."

"You didn't recognize either of us, did you?"

"I was only conscious of that van standing at the curb and of the nurse. I was frantic!"

"Would you like to tell me how you escaped and the truth of that trumped-up story about losing your belongings? And why, after making good your escape, would you have come back to Glendale and appealed to the sheriff?"

Rae measured him for a long moment, tempted to tell him the truth about herself and the real Dina. Then, because he returned her gaze so frankly and accepted her so sincerely as the real Dina, she reneged on the impulse and, to change the subject, said, "You were right about Pick."

This brought him alert, and his expression changed. "You've discovered something?"

She went on to relate the conversation with Pick in Mr. Boulleray's study with all its implications and near-implications. "He was like a wild man, Martin! I was actually afraid of him.

If Grandfather hadn't come in at that moment, I don't know what he might have done." She rubbed her forearms, her face haggard. "And he hates you. He thinks that you—you and I— are in love."

"Are we, Dina?" The bold question came in a steady tone.

The world rocked, and Rae, her eyes clinging to his, felt a spinning sensation as though she were going into orbit. "I—why do you ask me that?"

He deliberately turned his attention to the cooling coffee. "We had a lot of dreams once— young, sweet, crazy dreams—but nothing like this. *You* were nothing like this! That day when you ran to the car, I hoped you were running to me, and I would have defended you, Dina, for old times' sake. But that feeling was nothing like this. Now I've got to know!"

She floundered and, weak with longing, reached out to him. He took her hand and turned it palm up and kissed it. Her nerves tingled at his touch, and she thought insanely, *This is the second time in the last hour that someone has declared his love for me!*

Still holding her hand and toying with the fingers, he regarded her tenderly and repeated,

"I've got to know, Dina."

Eyes and cheeks glowed with her discovery. How long had she felt like this, not knowing? Why had she not seen it all along, this sweet rapport that she had dismissed as friendship for a likeable fellow? Friendship? Ah no, it was much more than that—an incredible attraction from the very first. But the ghastly truth smote her savagely. It was the other Dina he loved. "I'm going to have to go away from here, Martin. You know nothing about me."

"I know it was kid stuff then," he said generously. "But this—this is something else. I can't sleep for thinking about you—can't eat. When you didn't write—well, I wasn't exactly all broken up about that. There's a lot on a fella's mind out there. But when I saw you again, and you smiled at me, I decided that it needed looking into—I had to make a re-evaluation. When you sought me out, I waited for you to say something—something personal. It seemed better, on second thought, to play it by ear—to get acquainted again first."

Rae sat very still, trying to remember that it was Dina Boulleray to whom he was saying these things, to whom he was baring his heart. She felt that she was eavesdropping on something she had no right to hear, and a terrible enviousness seized her, shaming her with its hot breath. She couldn't bear to raise her eyes to his and see the love in them. Her fingers on the arm of the chair were icy and damp.

"Martin, there is so much I must tell you. I'm not what you think and—"

"Just the dearest, sweetest, loveliest girl in the world," he murmured broodingly. "I'd made up my mind to tell you the day I was hit. You touched my face after Greg kicked me, and it was like electricity going through me, honest. I was up there over the garage, holding a cold cloth to my face and laughing like a hyena with the joy of it. I stopped the bleeding and put on a clean shirt, and I kept saying, 'This is it! As soon as I get that damn motor running, I'll go get her and take her somewhere and tell her.' "

Rae winced. Cold waves of fear replaced the hot winds of shame. Had she found all this only to lose it? She rose and went blindly to the window to look unseeingly at the browning lawn, the drooping flowers bitten by frost. All that had happened, might not it be providential? Surely the other Dina could never be to this stalwart, handsome, kind young man what she, Rae, could be.

"Look at me, Dina!" he demanded with a lover's impatience.

She turned slowly, her eyes eloquent with all that was warring inside her. He saw what he wanted to see and moved close beside her to draw her to him. "I love you, darling," he whispered before he bent to kiss her. The kiss deepened, and she raised her arms to hold him to her, drowned in a sea of ecstasy.

"Darling, darling," she echoed. "Oh, Martin!"

Somewhere in the distance, the door chimes pealed three musical notes. Rae clung to him heedlessly. "I've never been in love before," she whispered against his mouth. "It hurts—terribly!"

His laugh was indulgent, triumphant, rich and warm. "Nor have I—never like this—never with a forevermore. Tell me again, you wonderful woman, that you love me."

Breathless, eyes sparkling, she leaned against him, laughing. "Where have I been?" she asked in wonderment. "That day at the hospital I knew there was something. I was so restless and miserable—so unhappy. Oh, Martin, I'm so *stupid!*"

He was smiling down at her in his arms, their faces very close, when there was an interruption,

"Dina, there's someone to see you," Pick announced gruffly.

She came back to reality and strained her eyes into the darkness of the hall. The shape of the man coming toward her was familiar—all too familiar!

"I've come to get you, Rae. Come on; we're getting out of here!"

CHAPTER TEN

Afterward Rae could hardly recall the sequence. She had felt physically ill, and resentment shook her until she wanted to shriek and pound her fists into the wall. She had clawed at Val's fingers, holding her wrist in a vise and dragging her to the front door. She remembered Martin saying, "Just a damn minute!" and an argument ensuing between the three men. Val said, "She sent for me. I have every right to take her—don't try to stop me!"

Half an hour later she was watching the blinking red of his taillights as he drove away without her, fuming with wrath. Inside, she encountered Woody coming down the massive staircase in terrible agitation.

"It's your grandfather, dearie! He's had a stroke."

Rae ran up the steps without another thought.

She heard Woody telephoning the doctor from the lower hall as she burst into Mr. Boulleray's room. Pick was with him, standing over him, his round face red with some inexplicable emotion. *And he was singing!*

Mr. Boulleray lay on the bed where Pick had laid him, fully clothed. Rae began to take off his shoes, and Pick interrupted himself in a bar of *Madam Butterfly* to protest. "Don't touch him!"

"But he looks so uncomfortable."

"Let him alone, you Jezebel!"

His eyes were blazing with wrath again, and she took her hands away. Mr. Boulleray lay in a queer position, his left side straight and stiff. His mouth worked spasmodically, although no words came. "He can't talk!" she sobbed.

"Get out! You did this to him with your men. Go away!"

"All right, but just until the doctor comes."

"*Stay* out!"

She waited in the corridor, perplexed and frightened, until Mrs. Wood and Grimes came up the stairs. "Dr. Albright's bringing a specialist," Mrs. Wood said hurriedly. "You get downstairs and break the news to Mrs. Shelby when she comes home. Try to keep her and

Greg downstairs until the doctors can talk to her. She's apt to upset the old man."

"Do as she says," Grimes admonished her. "We'll manage without you."

Rae knew herself to be banished—disgraced. There was no time to explain or to try to justify Val's sudden appearance and proprietary manner. She sat down on the steps to await Olivia's return, going over the puzzling scene with drooping spirits.

Val had yanked her to the car and tried to force her inside while she struggled. "You sent for me," he accused her, "and I'm taking you home. My wife and I had a hell of a battle about all this, and you're going to explain to her. Beely's been crying for days, and I hadn't the groggiest notion what was wrong with her until this morning when she unloaded it all. Now get in!"

"I can't, Val, I can't! I can't go away now, don't you see, when I've found my happiness?"

"Now listen. You told Beely that you were in terrible danger—being detained against your will by that big gorilla in there."

"I know, I know," Rae wailed. "But that was before."

"Before what?"

"Oh, Val, I can't explain it in a few words. It's too fantastic—too involved. You go home and tell Beely thank you—thank *you*, too, for coming! The whole situation has changed now. Oh, please go!"

He shook his head in puzzled concern. "I don't like this: you way out here miles from nowhere, that big guy wrestling me around. I tell you, Rae, I wouldn't have come except that— well, we meant a lot to each other once," he said virtuously, gallantly. "I couldn't let you down."

She could have screamed at the irony of it all. "I'll be all right, Val," she repeated. "I have someone now who cares. I'm sorry, so sorry, that I put you to this trouble."

"My God! That's all you have to say to me, after I left my wife in hysterics and drove like a bat out of hell all this distance?"

"That's all I *can* say, Val. I'm sorry, and thank you."

He got into the car, slamming the door angrily and swearing. Evidently Mr. Boulleray had had his stroke in the interim, and Pick had been in attendance. She must tell Martin now, tell him who she really was and why she had come there. Would he understand, or was it Dina Boulleray whom he loved? Just as soon as Olivia came she would go in search of him. And where was Greg? It was much too dark now to be riding the moors. Had he been thrown from his horse? Would ill luck never cease stalking this house and its inhabitants?

Dr. Albright arrived and, with him, a squat, swarthy little man whom he introduced as Dr. Alexander. Rae showed them to the sickroom and saw that the patient had been undressed and was lying in a coma under the bedclothes. She did not linger. There were still Olivia and Greg to inform.

They came in together, Olivia pantomiming the events of her day gaily, Greg charmingly attentive, both of them carefree. It was some time before Rae could engage their attention. After she had given them an account of the affliction, she asked them to wait for the doctors' verdict in the drawing room and went down the back hall to Martin's room.

He was not there.

"His room was empty when I came down to get supper," the cook said. "Maybe Letty knows."

Letty had gone to her own home across the meadow. Rae hesitated to pursue her for any

information she might have, although she would
have enjoyed a brisk walk in the frosty moonlit
night.

"What time are they going to expect supper?"
Cook asked. "Will those doctors stay, or what?"

"Trays, I think, for Mrs. Shelby and Greg
in their rooms. I imagine there'll be a nurse
shortly, and whether she'll have eaten or not,
I haven't the faintest idea."

"Which leaves me exactly nowhere. Here I
am with grilled salmon filets, not knowing when
to put them on."

"I'm sure Mrs. Wood will be down presently.
Do you think he might have gone to his place
above the garage?"

"Who?"

"Martin."

"Oh, him! I don't know."

Rae bit her lower lip uncertainly. Perhaps it
would be wiser to let him have a cooling-off
period before she made her confession. Then
she would tell him the whole truth and take the
consequences. If Pick thought her a "Jezebel,"
might not Martin, too? If only Val had not come
to her rescue on that particular day at such a
significant moment. She went into the drawing
room to do what she could for Olivia.

"Just tell me, please, what went on around her today." Olivia was pacing the floor and drawing a silk handkerchief through her fingers. "What did Father do before it happened?"

"He had his nap," Rae said, "and came down to the study about four. I left him with Pick to go over some papers."

"You didn't speak to him?"

"Yes, I mentioned that I had come in there for my book, and he said to take good care of Martin."

Greg was watching her closely. "That was all?"

"He said something about Martin being a remarkable person and worthy of his ancestry."

"Ha!" Greg sneered.

"And where were you when Father was stricken?" Mrs. Shelby asked.

"I was outside saying goodbye to a friend."

Olivia's lucid brown eyes livened with interest. "You had a caller? Who?"

"A man from Seattle," Rae said shortly. They would soon know, all of them, that she was an impostor, so let them fit the pieces together any way they chose.

Woody came to the door and sighed in relief when she saw Rae. "Your grandpa wants you, dearie. They gave him something to make him sleep, so you better hurry. Mrs. Shelby, Dr. Albright and Dr. Alexander are coming right down. Do you want me to bring in cocktails and set two extra places for dinner?"

"I don't see why Father would ask for Dina," Olivia complained. "When did he get his power of speech back?"

Woody gave Rae a little shove. "Hurry, dear. Well, Mrs. Shelby, he just said one word— 'Deeno,' like he used to call her. The doctor said to humor him until the sedative took effect."

That was all Rae heard. The doctors were taking their leave as she went upstairs. She found Grimes alone with Mr. Boulleray. She went to the bedside and leaned close to the old man to hear him.

"Don't go, Deen," he rasped. "Don't let them—"

She looked at Grimes questioningly. "He has some idea that you are going away," Grimes said. "If you could reassure him—"

Rae's eyes filled with tears, and she held the cold parchment hands in her warm ones. "I won't leave you, Grandfather—ever."

This satisfied him, apparently. He nodded and patted her hand. "Good girl!"

She waited until he was asleep, the sound of his heavy breathing filling the room. "What did the doctors say?" she asked Grimes.

"Only a light stroke. He was beginning to come out of it by the time they came."

"Are they sending a nurse?"

"No, I'll take care of him as I've always done," he said softly. "I've been with him for a long time, Miss Dina."

"May I stay for a while, in case he wants me again?"

"No, you go have your dinner. I'll fetch you if you're needed."

To escape the confusion downstairs, Rae went to her room to freshen up. Olivia would be holding court for another hour before dinner, from the sound of it. She brushed her hair and selected a plain periwinkle wool from Dina's well-stocked closet. How sad that none of these pretty clothes had gone with the girl to Morely's Institute. Had they kept her in restraint? How awful! She brushed her face with powder and added fresh lipstick to her mouth. The worst of her fright had passed now, and she could be calm. She went down the back stairs to help Woody and Cook with the late dinner. By the time the guests came across the hall, she was

composed and serene. Pick was not with them.
Dr. Albright complimented her on her appearance as he held her chair, and she thanked him
absently.

"Dina is a protégée of mine," he said to Dr.
Alexander when they were all seated. "Remarkable improvement. One of the cases that makes
it all worth-while."

The doctor gave her a shrewd, piercing glance
across the table. "Your grandfather appears to
be devoted to you, Miss Boulleray."

Olivia coughed significantly. "My poor
brother's orphaned child—very sad! We've all
tried—done everything, you know. My Greg was
just a little tot when we came home. His father
and I are divorced. And Dina had been spoiled
by Father—"

"Mother!" Greg reminded her.

"Oh, I'm always getting scolded for recalling
the past," she simpered. "Doctor, do try this
lemon butter on your salmon. Dina, where is
Pick?"

"I don't know."

"He went out shortly after we came," Dr.
Albright said. "I was sorry not to have had an
opportunity to speak to him. He seemed distraught."

"Such a shock," Olivia said, "to have been with Father when he was stricken."

Rae had an odd sinking sensation. Dr. Albright and Pick—hadn't Martin hinted that day at the hospital that they might be allies in the hope of mutual gain?

"How is Martin after his accident?" Dr. Albright asked.

"Ask Dina," Greg blurted out hoarsely. "She has elected herself his nurse."

"He is improving satisfactorily, Doctor."

"Young, lovely, and with the light shining seductively on her dusky hair, she returned his gaze candidly.

"These relationships have me confused," Dr. Alexander said in his thick accent. "The mother and the boy and this granddaughter—I know them. But who are these others?"

"Pickeral Nichols is our estate manager, Doctor, and no relation. Martin used to be a neighbor boy on an adjoining estate. After his service in Vietnam he was disoriented. My father takes in people like that. Martin has been our chauffeur and mechanic lately, and recently he met with an accident. Fortunately, Dr. Albright was here at the time. He is home from the hospital now, recuperating."

"What kind of accident?"

There was a stealthy pause before Dr. Albright said tightly, "Someone hit him over the head with a wrench—concussion." He looked solemnly at Rae. "Has his memory returned?"

"His memory is perfect, Doctor," she said coolly. "His assailant struck him from behind, so naturally he can't identify him."

"Probably some itinerant," Greg broke in. "We have them all the time during the harvest season."

"Martin's inclined to be quarrelsome," Olivia interjected. "He may have ordered him off the premises too roughly."

Rae rose. "If you'll excuse me, I'll sit with Grandfather while Grimes has his dinner. Good night, Dr. Albright. Nice to have met you, Dr. Alexander."

As the men resumed their seats, she heard Dr. Alexander say, "An admirable young lady— such poise and presence."

"Oh, our Dina can be a tigress when she wants," Olivia said with a tinkling laugh, "can't she, Dr. Albright?"

The entrance hall and staircase were dimly lighted, and Rae paused to draw a long breath, glad to escape the deceptive conversation and its intimations. A "poor orphan," was she? And Martin was maladjusted? Oh, Olivia had the reins now, and she would throw herself into the farce with all her skill. Only Greg and Pick would emerge unscathed by her scurrilous innuendo.

Grimes welcomed her with dignity and went down the back hall to the kitchen. She moved about softly, unable to sit still. A fine rain clung to the windowpanes, and the raw roaring sound of the waterfall seemed louder than ever in the quiet of the room. She dared not let herself think of Martin and all that had passed between them in that brief interlude. That path would lead to madness in the mood she was in now.

"Oh, how can I endure it?" she whispered to the silent walls. "Never to see him again—never to know the glorious fulfillment of love!"

She bowed her head in her hands and wept while the old man lay sleeping.

CHAPTER ELEVEN

Pick had not returned by the end of the week. Nor had Rae seen Martin.

She established herself in the sickroom with Grimes, leaving only when he insisted that she take a walk or rest in her room. Mr. Boulleray said little, the effort to speak being almost too much for him, but he kept her hand in his while she sat beside him, smiling contentedly or dozing.

On one of her afternoon walks, she thought she saw Martin spinning out through the gates in the small car which was used for errands. So he was still on the premises! That meant that he had purposely avoided her all this time. Her thoughts were perplexing and irresolute as she pondered all that had happened. She couldn't leave now, with Mr. Boulleray depending on her so much, nor did she pursue her plan to confess all to Martin. Since he felt so resentful toward her, she cringed from the idea of telling all to him and having him repulse her further. To explain Val, she would have to say that she had phoned him to come, and that would damn her for sure.

The woods were sere now, reminding her that winter was not far off. If she had had any money or any means of transportation at all, she might have cut out. She had a wild impulse to get away, to flee from any chance encounter with Martin and the sight of scorn in those eyes which had been so tender for a little while.

There was the sound of a horse's hooves on the bridle trail to her left, and she turned to see Greg rein in beside her. "I've noticed you don't ride any more," he said querulously. "Could it be that you're afraid?"

"It could be. You'll recall I'm a little out of practice."

His steed pawed the ground restlessly, and he gave it rein, calling over his shoulder, "It won't do you any good to cater to Gramps, you know. He's pretty well soured on you."

Rae watched him down the trail, almost hating him and his arrogance. Mr. Boulleray was not "soured" on her, no matter how deftly Olivia and Pick had tried to achieve this result. He clung to her and, in his feeble way, indicated that her presence was most welcome. What had changed him? she wondered. Something had happened that last day before his attack when he had been alone with Pick—something to bring on a stroke? Pick had been so ready to accuse her, but mightn't *he* have said or done something? Certainly he had made himself scarce since the old man's illness.

Her musings drifted back to that rain-lashed night when she had picked up an untidy waif at the side of the road, the night when this whole sequence of events had begun. Dina Boulleray! Where was she now, and what had she done in the past to set Greg and Olivia against her? Everyone seemed to have a different scale on which to measure the girl. Woody and her grandfather loved her, Pickeral Nichols wanted her for himself, and the Shelbys hated her. What about Martin? He had intimated that he'd always been fond of her when they were children together, and he'd said as he held Rae in his arms, "But nothing like this!" Which of them did he really and truly love—Rae or Dina? Oh, it was all too hideous, this comedy of errors which was drawing them all into a web of hatred and mistrust! If only she could discuss it with Mr. Boulleray, relieving herself of the burden and depending on his wisdom and good judgment. If only she had Martin back, loving her and believing in her!

A cold wind had risen off the sea, chilling her through by the time she reached the house. She went in through the kitchen, the warmth welcome to her frozen hands and feet, and paused beside the big glowing stove to let the coziness seep into her. Although Cook was nowhere about, there was something delicious baking in the oven. Rae lingered, sniffing the fragrance, and was tempted to peek. She heard Woody's voice coming from the room which had been prepared for Martin.

"You can't ask this of me, son!" she said in a voice throbbing with horror. "Not even for you—no. Besides, he hasn't said anything—not a word."

"He will, Mother, he will!" The voice was Pick's. "He has only tolerated me all these years on your account."

"You and Dina will make up, dearie, and when you're married everything will be just as we planned all along."

"Never!" he said fervently. "I despise her!

It would be like taking an asp to my bosom. She's a Magdalene, scarlet and soiled, sinful and defiled."

Mother? Son? Rae stood motionless as their voices shifted into murmurings. And she married to Pick? No, no! She was afraid of him, mortally afraid! Hadn't he as much as admitted that he had cracked Martin's skull because of her? Somewhere inside that enormous expanse of brawn and muscle was a tiger which, if unleashed by pride or jealousy, would be bent to kill. Oh, dear heaven, what had she done to direct his animosity toward *her?* And, more to the point, what did he want his mother to do to Mr. Boulleray? Doubly alerted now, she stole quietly from the kitchen to the only room where she felt safe in this house of horrors—to Mr. Boulleray's sickroom.

Grimes was there, nodding over the evening farm journal. He, at least, seemed normal, his thinning hair shining under the table light, his face etched with lines of kindness. She spoke to him softly in order not to disturb the patient.

"Grimes, are you and I the only ones who attend my grandfather?"

His high forehead wrinkled in mystification at the blunt question. "Surely, Miss Dina, you know that."

"Yes, but I mean, don't Mrs. Wood and Letty do the cleaning or anything?"

"I've always kept Mr. Boulleray's room clean and attended to his person and clothes," he assured her loftily.

She remembered just in time that she should have known this as the "other" Dina. "What I was wondering," she amended, "is who prepares his food."

"Why, I do, now that he is on a strict diet. Most of it comes from cans—those little baby food cans. A bland diet. Are you implying that I starve him?"

"No, certainly not! I just wondered, that's all." If poison was the instrument, Mrs. Wood would have little opportunity. *But Pick wanted the old man out of the way!* He seemed to have *no* illusions about the old man's regard for him, and he—what *did* he intend to do to insure his own position as manager of financial affairs of the Boullery interests? Now that he recoiled from marriage with her, the "Magdalene," the "Jezebel," what would his next step be? She wanted to ask Grimes if Pick had been in the room since his return, but thought better of it. Perhaps he had made a quick visit to his mother to enlist her aid in his nefarious scheme and would go away again. That would mean only one enemy to police instead of two. And that one enemy was, of all people, Mrs. Wood! It didn't seem possible that the rosy-cheeked, forthright little woman could be an accessory to possible murder. Did Grimes know that she and Pick were mother and son? She thought not. Mr. Boulleray must know, though, for Pick had said that the old man only tolerated him because of Mrs. Wood. Oh, it was too ugly and confusing to think of the darling old man surrounded by enemies in his own household!

That neither Olivia nor Greg had been allowed to see him, she was certain. And from Greg's snide remark that afternoon, she knew, too, that they resented *her* welcome presence in the sickroom. Somehow, though, she couldn't believe that either of them would deliberately harm the old man.

Mr. Boulleray stirred, and she went to his bedside. Taking his hand, she said, "Is there anything you want, Grandfather? Anything I can do for you?"

"Denno?"

"Yes, Grandfather, I'm here."

"Don't go," he managed to gurgle.

"No, I'll stay right here—here with you."
She was so stirred that tears filled her eyes.

"He's sorely distressed about something,"
Grimes said from his chair. "Perhaps he wants
the bed pan."

"No—no!" Mr. Boulleray gasped. "Deen—"
Rae sat beside him, holding his cold hands
in hers and moved by his devotion. "I'll be here,"
she choked, "always." Be quiet now, dear, so
you can get your strength back." Remembering
Pick singing to him the other day, she began
a tuneless little humming and was relieved to
see him smile contentedly.

"I wonder if I could have a cot put up in the
parlor," she said to Grimes when he was asleep.
Grimes' own cot was set up in the bedroom.
"If he should waken during the night and want
me—"

"That's a splendid idea," he agreed, to her
surprise. "The couch in there is comfortable, and
he—I'm sure he'd like the arrangement. You're
very kind-hearted, Miss Dina." His clear eyes
measured her briefly, and he added, "Very
changed."

"Oh, come now," she chided him lightly.
"Have I been so beastly in the past?"

"You've caused him much sorrow," he said

quietly. "You can't deny that."

Again, Rae had the uncomfortable sensation of being blamed for the deeds of another. "I'm so sorry about everything," she said humbly. "I want to make it up to him if I can. I love him dearly, Grimes."

The man's face relaxed into affection. "You're doing that. We've talked about—well, to be truthful, about you. He—I think for a while he thought you to be guilty of that attack on Martin and trying to blame it on Greg. Then when you were so good to the boy and nursed him the way you did—he's fair, you know—we both knew that you'd changed."

What was Dina Boulleray? Rae wondered. *Waif or beast?* There had been many references to her bad temper, her violence, but surely the child had been provoked into these acts. She wished Grimes would go on talking and clarify these deeds, but he had opened his paper again and was studying the stock market. Rae replenished the fire in the parlor and suggested that he rest until dinner. He agreed gratefully, and she was left alone with her thoughts. A prisoner with only the company of two old men, she told herself, their heavy breathing filling the room like the sighs of death. Alone in a locked room and helpless. If Martin knew of her predicament, might he not offer some protection? The hours dragged by while the wind howled at the chimney in grim monotony and the naked branches of the trees scratched against the windows with ghostly fingers. Was Pick still in the quiet house, and how would Mrs. Wood carry out her promise to her son? Her head whirled at the presence of evil, and there was no one to whom she could turn. Thank God, though, that she had been alerted!

Mr. Boulleray roused for his dinner, which Grimes had prepared and fed to him. Rae left the room while Mr. Boulleray was being made comfortable for the night. Presently the dinner gong would sound, and she must order her and Grimes' meals sent up from below. The barricade would begin! She slipped down the hall to her own room to gather a few garments for the night—and found Mrs. Wood there!

"I was just turning down your bed, dearie, and fixing your fire. It's turned nasty out. I shouldn't be surprised if it rained."

Rae was so filled with revulsion that she could hardly speak to the woman. "I shan't be sleeping here tonight," she said tightly. "My grandfather wants me with him. Will you please bring me bed linens and blankets from the closet?"

"Now what's the sense in that?" Mrs. Wood protested. "You get your good night's sleep, dearie. Grimes will look after him."

"Grandfather wants me," Rae replied adamantly. "Also, Grimes and I will dine in the suite, so please arrange with Cook for trays, will you?"

"Well, now, that's going to take a bit of doing," Mrs. Wood demurred. "With trouble in the house, there's a certain amount of bad humor. Why can't Grimes eat in the kitchen the way he always does? Cook's not going to care for this extra work."

"That's just too bad," Rae retorted rudely. "Now, if you'll bring the bedding, please."

Mrs. Wood trotted away disconsolately, and presently Rae heard the gong sound and knew that the others were assembling without her. Let them wonder and fuss and conjecture; she had made one solemn vow during the long afternoon, and that was to protect her grandfather at all costs.

She packed night clothes and a few essentials in her cosmetics case and, annoyed that Mrs. Wood had not returned from her errand, went to the hall closet to obtain all that she would need for the couch. The clock downstairs struck seven.

She assembled the paraphernalia and went to the bookcase beside the window for a couple of books with which to pass the evening hours. A new magazine caught her eye, and she opened it to peruse the glossy pictures. The skirts were longer now, making her and Dina's wardrobes out of style. Ah well, what difference did it make?

The waterfall splashed and gurgled down over the tall rocks, and over its sound she heard something else—a cry like that of a cat or animal. She peered into the darkness, curious and startled. There was no access to her room from that side unless one dared to risk crawling under the falls to climb up those slippery black crags.

And someone had!

Fascinated, she watched as the figure swung out from the mists and proceeded cautiously to the window, then leaped back as her own reflection came into hazy view.

"Open the window! Let me in!"

The visitor, coming like a thief in the night, was Dina Boulleary!

CHAPTER TWELVE

Rae was torn between pity for the wet and bedraggled girl and concern for the condition of her own best winter coat, which hung about Dina in rags. She saw, too, that the girl was as pale and thin, as unkempt and shabby as she had been that first night when it had all begun. She looked exhausted beyond the power of speech as she flopped into a chair, breathing hard.

"How is my grandfather?" she asked after an interval to regain her breath.

"He has been ill—a stroke of some kind—but he is improving. Now, Celia,—I mean Dina—we must get you into a hot bath and dry clothes or you'll be sick. Get out of those wet things while I run the water for you."

First things first! Questions were boiling inside her, but her previous experience with the girl told her that she would speak only when she was ready and once more comfortable. *I seem always to be urging her to bathe and dry off*, she thought wryly. Where had she come from, and why? Surely she couldn't have heard of Mr. Boulleray's illness on her travels. When Dina was in the bath, Rae gingerly lifted the soggy coat and sighed. She had purchased the fine garment nearly a year ago at one of Seattle's posh small shops in anticipation of a Saturday luncheon party with some of Val's college friends. Less than a year ago? It seemed an eternity!

"I'll be so proud of you, darling. I want to show you off and have them all envy me."

And so she had paid far too much for the mink-trimmed red cashmere and gone with Val to the elegant Olympic Hotel, where she was toasted and praised and admired by the other young men, much to Val's delight. Her mouth twisted ruefully. A lot of good it had done when dear Beely came bursting back on the scene. Now the coat was a wreck. She debated what to do with it and the other things that Dina had carelessly discarded on the carpet. There were wet splotches on the light green rug and on the chair where Dina had sat. Rae bundled the gar-

ments up into a roll and thrust them far back
in her closet to avoid Mrs. Wood's questions.
She debated how to get Dina something to eat
without arousing the curiosity of the household.
First, she must ascertain whether Dina wished
to remain incognito or to appear before the
family. In the latter case, the cat would surely
be out of the bag! She laid out a warm wool robe
and pajamas, hoping that Dina would go to
bed and wait until morning to make an appearance. Rae had to guard Mr. Boulleray tonight
from whatever threat hung over him. Tomorrow?
Tomorrow she would be free! She'd take her
car and set out for somewhere—anywhere. With
Dina home again, it would be too embarrassing
to stay.

Again Dina came from the bathroom, her
hair loose, and Rae was struck anew by the
remarkable resemblance between them. Dina was
pitifully thin, but her pale face bore traces of
color from the steam and the warmth. Rae lit
the fire Mrs. Wood had laid and helped the girl
into the big comfortable bed.

"I'll have to leave you for a moment, Dina,
to look after your grandfather. Then I'll come
back, and we must talk."

"I know you're mad," Dina said pettishly,

"and I guess I can't blame you. But if you had been in my place, with that stinky nurse Celia and Dr. Albright breathing down your neck, you'd have done the same thing."

"I *was* in your place," Rae said grimly, "and they breathed down *my* neck."

Dina clapped her hands together like a child. "Oh, what fun! How did they catch you?"

"That's another story and one which we will go into later. Now snuggle down and keep warm until I come back."

"And bring something to eat," Dina ordered imperiously. "I'm starved."

Little brat, Rae thought disparagingly as she carried her gear to the sickroom. She was beginning to understand fully why the child was regarded so unfavorably. Now what did she have up her little cotton-picking sleeve?

Grimes was finishing his dinner when she unlocked the door and shot the bolt. "Thoughtful of you, Miss Dina. You'd better eat; your food's getting cold."

Rae nodded toward the sickroom. "Still asleep? I think I'll take mine to my room. There are a few things that need my attention."

"He's had a sleeping pill, so take your time."

"Who brought up the meals?"

"Letty. Nice youngster. Says they're keeping her on permanently."

Good! That would be one more loyal person to call upon if help was needed. She instructed Grimes about bolting the door after her and, with all the stealth of an international spy, crept along the long corridor with her tray to where Dina was waiting for her. The girl fell on the food like a hungry alley cat, licking her lips and glancing anxiously at Rae from time to time. "Good!" She grinned through mouthfuls. "Is there any more?"

"No, and that's my supper you just inhaled. Now, Dina, I want you to tell me everything— where you've been all this time and why you came back. No tricks this time, hear?"

"Nobody talks to me like that!" the girl pouted.

"Well, maybe you don't usually have to face your victims. You've caused me no end of trouble, and I have every right. Now, first of all, where is my car?"

This struck home. Dina peeked out from the drying strands of dark hair falling about her face and said, "I'm sorry about that—honestly. It just conked out—you know what a lousy driver I am—and I've had to walk miles and miles."

She gulped the last of her tea and went on, "All right, I'll tell you. First I went to Portland, Oregon. I had some idea of losing myself in a city, and I had your money and everything I needed. It was pretty stale there, so I struck out for San Francisco. I thought maybe I could get a job. But gosh, all the things you have to know, and all those questions on the application blanks! I guess I don't know much about working."

"I guess you don't," Rae said crisply. "I guess you don't know much about the penalties for using another person's credit cards and stealing, either. Do you know that I had a good job waiting for me which you ruined? Or that I was on the ragged edge of being socked back into Morely's Institute in your place? Now where did you leave my car and all my luggage?"

Dina picked at her lower lip and had the grace to be embarrassed. "I sold them. Well-ll," she whined unhappily as Rae glared, "I ran out of money, and I was homesick for Gimpy. I went to a Salvation Army place—that shows you how hard up I was—and they talked about the Prodigal Son and how he was welcomed home, and I cried. It was rough getting back, I'll tell you! Most of the time I hitchhiked; the rest

I had to walk."

"Didn't you think of being apprehended when you got to Glendale?"

"Yes, some. I had your credentials, though, and I figured I could tell them I was you, see?"

"Why didn't you just ring the doorbell and announce your return instead of risking your life on those boulders out there?"

"Oh, I wasn't afraid," Dina said airily. "I used to come in that way lots of times. And the reason I didn't come in the front way was because of Pick and Woody." She swore briefly and with practiced art. "I couldn't risk that mangy Pick taking me back there again."

"Pick did that? I thought he was in love with you."

"So did I, the big hunk of blubber; That's why I trusted him. I never did like him, and I used to tease him, but I *did* trust him. Woody, too, the little fat snake!"

Rae glanced at her watch, the one thing Dina had left her when she split. "I haven't much time left, Dina, but I must know why they did such a cruel thing to you. Didn't your grandfather interfere? Surely you trusted *him*."

"Oh, I was young then," she said nonchalantly, "and Gimpy bugged me. He was so strict, never letting me have the car or go any place, always trying to make a lady of me—" she gave a harsh laugh—"and a Christian. That was Preacher Pick's department, the big phony. I got blamed, too, for everything Greg did. I hated them all, and I told them so. That was when Pick took me over to Morely's—to take the sass out of me, he said, so I'd be a proper wife for a preacher. Oh, he and Woody were pretty smooth about it until I got there. Cooping me up like a wild animal! Wouldn't you hate them, too?"

"But you came back."

"Yeah, I had a lot of time to think—about Gimpy, that is. And I decided that if he knew the truth, knew that Pick was always drooling over me and wanting me to marry him—I had to be old enough, though, so Gramps couldn't object. So there was only one thing to do if I didn't want to *really* go crazy, and that was to cut out. I made up to a dim-wit named Curt who was a trusty. That's how I got the van, and I scrammed. The minute I saw you, I knew my luck was holding."

"And mine had just run out the minute I glimpsed you."

"Oh, indubitably—a sketch!"

"And you've fooled them all? All this time?"
Dina's tone was rich with the admiration of one
conspirator for another. "I've got to hand it
to you. Does Gimpy buy it, too?"

"He remarks often on how I've changed,"
Rae said sharply. "And so do the others." She
shook her head accusingly. "You must have
been a stupid idiot, Dina."

"Well, like Gimpy said, I was high-spirited,"
Dina admitted proudly. "And after I got that
split skull from a fall from my pony, I seemed
to get worse. I'm all right now, though, except
I'm sleepy and still hungry."

"Where does Martin fit into all this?"

"Martin? Oh yes, the war veteran. Well, for
a while he lived with his folks over the hill—
just a kid—and he used to defend me against
that nasty little Greg. Then when he was grown,
he went away. That was the last I saw of him."

"You're not in love with him?"

"How could I be? I haven't seen him in years.
He wrote once or twice, but you know how it is."

"Yes, I'm beginning to see," Rae said thoughtfully.

Dina yawned widely. "So that's the story.
You'll have to get the money from Gimpy for
your car and stuff."

"That's not the entire story, I'm sorry to say, Dina. Your grandfather is partially paralyzed from a stroke. He can't talk or see anyone except Grimes and me. Also, I have reason to believe there is a plot against his life."

Dina bolted upright from her pillows. "Oh, no!"

"Yes, and it's very devious. His health is precarious, too, and he must be spared any shock at present. Which means, my dear little thief, that you are again in captivity right here in this room."

"I don't care! I'd like to sleep for a week. By that time he'll be well."

"Its not quite that simple, I'm afraid. Since you don't want to see any of the other members of the household, you'll have to trust me implicitly. And I insist that you stay in this room, door locked and seeing no one, until your grandfather is well enough to be acquainted with the facts."

"Well, I must say you're awfully bossy for an impostor," Dina flared. "That's why I ran away in the first place—all that bossing around."

"But now you're back, and the rule still holds. Grin and bear it!" Rae said flippantly. "I'm going to lock your door from the outside in case Woody comes snooping around, and I advise you to secure the bolt when I'm gone. See you in the morning."

"Not before noon, I hope. I'm dead!"

Rae sat late before the fire after Grimes had retired, sorting out the things Dina had said. Her own position was even more complicated now. Not only would she be exposed as an impostor, but Dina had junked the car, making escape impossible. This was a gloomy old house with tragedy stalking it, yet for a little while it had been home to her and the old man lying in there who was so incredibly dear to her heart. There were the complications, too, engendered by her feeling for Martin. He might take one of two stands in regard to her unofficial status there—complete renunciation or the dawning acceptance of reality. If only she could talk to him, go over it all point by point and make him understand. Dina had denied being in love with him, so wasn't there the possibility that he had fallen in love with her, Rae, instead of Dina?

And another fact thrust itself into the fore of her musings: Dina hated Pick and Woody. This confirmed her own impression of Pick, but Woody, she had to confess, had fooled her completely until that afternoon. A doting mother,

the little woman had somehow become implicated in her son's desire to gain control of The
Knob by marrying its most prominent heiress.
That failing, they could easily dispose of the
aging and helpless owner and juggle the papers
which Pick handled to put him in full authority.
Even though there were the Shelbys to contend
with in such a scheme, what could the fluttery
little Olivia do but complain? Greg might be
someone to reckon with if he were older and
steadier, but again, like his mother, he was concerned only with his immediate comforts and
whims. There was no strength in either of them.

So I must stay, she thought raggedly. *I must
stay until the criminals make their pitch and
are exposed!*

CHAPTER THIRTEEN

No one in the house noticed anything amiss in the dark and rainy days that followed.

Rae drew courage from the fact that Mr. Boulleray was improving slowly and surely. He coud feed himself now, could joke mildly about his own helpless state when Grimes shaved him, and his speech was improving daily.

"Another day, Deeno, and a little sunshine will put me in shape. I warn you, I'll be able to trim you at canasta shortly."

"That'll be the day!" she scoffed fondly.

"Why is the house so quiet? Where is everyone?"

"Doing what the doctor ordered," she retorted, "and keeping quiet. Are you getting tired of Grimes and me?"

"Not you, my dear, never you! Grimes? Well, he's another pipeful of tobacco. He's my strong right arm."

Grimes allowed himself a slight smile in reply to the tribute. He was good and true, Rae thought, but hardly strong. During these past days she had wondered many times how they—Grimes, an old man, and herself, a girl—could defend Mr. Boulleray if the occasion presented itself. With this in mind, she had assembled a few weapons of protection which she secreted in the parlor of the suite—a baseball bat, splintered and cracked; the fire poker and iron tongs; a can of hair spray to blind the attacker temporarily. These she lined up at hand whenever Grimes was briefly absent to bring firewood or prepare the patient's meals. And another thing bothered her: Mr. Boulleray was no longer on the baby food diet. Someone could slip poison into the rich hearty soups and stews he was now enjoying. Grimes couldn't understand her concern about the food.

"This was already prepared, Grimes?"

"Sure. It'd been cooking for hours. All I had to do was dish it up."

"Cook prepared it?" Rae instinctively trusted Cook.

"Sure. She won't let anyone else near the stove of hers, you know that."

True, but how easy it would be for Mrs. Wood to put a potion in the bowl while Grimes wasn't looking.

One evening when Dina became feverish and nauseated after dinner, Rae was gravely concerned. She hesitated to summon Dr. Alexander and expose the child's presence, but she vowed to do so if it were warranted by morning.

"I ate too much, that's all," Dina assured her. "It's your fault for trying to fatten me up. I feel like I'm almost ready for the butcher."

"You're not nearly fat enough. You still look like a plucked chicken."

"And I'm always hungry." Dina giggled. "I guess I've got an eating complex from all those Salvation Army doughnuts. Golly, how I longed for a hamburger!"

Rae couldn't help feeling sorry for the girl, although she was becoming more and more of a problem. The extra food must be accounted for to Cook, and Rae blamed herself. "It's your good cooking," she said, "that makes me such a pig."

"Ah, go on with you! A slim slip of a girl like you!"

And Dina was becoming restless in the close confinement, too. "I want to see my horse and the old dog down at the stables."

"In this rain? Don't be silly! Someone would be sure to see you prowling about."

"I want to see Gimpy!"

"And bring on another stroke from shock? Listen, do you want to blow it all?"

Dina pouted. "Everybody can't be as efficient —and *officious*—as you, Rae. How long does this crazy deception go on? I could do all that you're doing for him."

"And what becomes of me?" Rae lashed out. "You've wrecked my life, stolen all that I own and run up debts on me—what do you propose that *I* do? Get lost out there in the rain?"

"You don't need to get so huffy about it!"

"Well, I *am* huffy!"

"Couldn't I just look at him while he's asleep?"

"Dina, I've told you that I think his life is in danger. Perhaps I should tell you why I believe this to be so." She went on then to relate the conversation she had overheard between Pick and Mrs. Wood. "They are mother and son, Dina. Did you know that?"

"No, but I can't say that I'm surprised. Woody was always so lenient with him, singing his praises the way Olivia does Greg's, never seeing anything wrong in what he did. Yes, I'll bet you are right! But what does that mean, after all? Pick wouldn't *kill* anyone, would he? He's a preacher."

"He almost killed Martin," Rae said, and saw the girl's eyes widen with shock. "For some reason he was jealous of Martin and me—you, rather." She told of the incident of Greg kicking Martin and of the aftermath when Martin was struck with the wrench. "They all thought I—you—did it. Dina. Whatever gave you such a reputation for violence? I've had to bear up under the stigma of your past behavior ever since I've been here."

"Oh, Rae, I've tried to explain it to you. That first night when you picked me up and saw we looked alike, I told you how I've always been— wanted to be—another person. I'd like to be like you, really."

"Now where did you get all this exaggerated ESP foolishness?" Rae asked in exasperation. Just when she was getting some sense out of the girl, her mood changed.

"I got it from Pick," Dina said without hesitation. "He tried to train me to be my 'other self' *all* the time, but I couldn't." She leaned forward earnestly. "This is the way it works, see. You're composed of good and evil—two distinct dispositions. You have to keep the bad stamped out so that the good can grow and flower. That's what he said, and Dr. Albright agreed with Pick, too. So you see, when I struck out with all your stuff, I *was* you. And that's how you became *me*."

"That's nonsense, pure unadulterated nonsense!" Rae exclaimed with warm indignation. "How could you let yourself be duped by such foolishness? Dina," she went on less irritably, "each of us is an individual, a complete entity in herself. Maybe we do have a mixture of good and bad in us, I grant you that, but we do not have *other selves!* I'm me, and you're *you!* I can't assume your identity, nor you mine. We're distinct from each other, except that we bear a remarkable resemblance when it comes to our facial features."

"Maybe we're twins, and you were secreted off to some other place for malicious reasons. Maybe they left you for dead, and a kind farmer came along in his donkey cart and raised you as his own child. I ready a story once where that happened. There was this prince, see, and his uncle—"

"—Coveted the throne. I read it, too, but I

assure you that my father was no farmer, nor I
a foundling. Our resemblance is merely a trick
of nature, one from which we must try to
extricate ourselves eventually when your grandfather recovers. Until then—"

"We're in a mess, aren't we?"

"We are," Rae acknowledged ruefully. "I don't
know how we can go on like this indefinitely.
Our first concern is, of course, your grandfather's recovery. The next is exposing Pick and
Woody. I don't know how that can be done, but
I *do* know that I'll protect Grandfather to the
last ditch."

"You love him, don't you?" Dina said wistfully.

Rae's face softened. "You don't know how
much!" she said ardently. She thought of her
love for Martin, too, and was tempted for a
moment to confide in the irresponsible girl whose
own desires took precedence over the rights of
others. "Dina, I don't know how you could have
used him so badly," she said reproachfully,
"when he loves you so dearly."

Dina pouted at the implied criticism. "You
forget that Gimpy allowed Pick to take me away
and that I spent two terrible years in that awful
place."

"No, I don't forget that, dear," Rae said with swift compassion. "It must have been terrible for you, hating restraint as you do."

"Caged! They kept me caged!" Dina was warming to her self-pity. "I counted the squares on the linoleum to keep from going bats. I said the multiplication tables over and over and made up stories." She twisted a lock of her hair depectedly. "And when Pick came—"

"He did come?"

Dina spat in disgust. "Oh, sure. He was on that soul-saving kick, like I told you, and Dr. Albright had him preaching to all of us about hell and damnation." She gave a lusty sigh. "I'm telling you, he could make it so real you could feel the *fire!* Not one word about God's love and mercy—just that damn hellfire! Oh, he was eloquent all right! Some of the patients used to scream for hours after he left."

"You, Dina?"

"I?" The girl gave a bitter laugh. "*I* was smarter than he and Doc Albright thought. I know what they both wanted from me."

"What was that?"

"The Knob."

"Of course! Pick wanted to marry you—break you down so that you'd be amenable to his scheme—but what was Dr. Albright's motive?"

"He had a stake, you can bet on that. A phony head-shrinker—why wouldn't he snap at the chance for a fat slice of dough? I used to get my kicks telling him I hated Pick and that I was in love with someone else—someone who would rescue me one day." She pulled her hair over her head and grinned through it impishly. "That really set them off—you wouldn't believe! *Who was he?* They kept at me for hours and hours. Finally I had to make up someone, so I thought of Martin!"

"Martin!" So that was why Pick hated Martin! It accounted, too, for Martin's concern for herself, Rae. Yet was he or was he not in love with the real Dina? Rae felt a wave of hope that kindled in her eyes and snatched away her breath. Martin had felt protective toward the wronged Dina, but could it be herself, Rae, that he had fallen in love with? She regarded Dina gravely. "You didn't care for Martin, though, did you?"

"Why do you keep harping on that?" Dina asked petulantly. " 'Course not.' He was just the only one I could think of, that's all."

And you almost cost him his life! Rae wanted to lash out at her. *You made Pick hate him and try to kill him!* The worst of it was, she thought wildly, that Pick would surely make another attempt to remove the man he supposed to be his rival. He had seen them kissing, Rae and Martin, that afternoon when Val had come. *Oh, I must warn Martin!* she thought. *I must explain to him about Dina, about me, and tell him everything!*

The first snow began to fall in the later afternoon. Softly it fell, like flower petals from a gray sky, until, at dusk, a cold wet wind came in from the sea, turning the flakes into tiny pellets of pounding ice. Rae, going from Mr. Boulleray's suite to her own room, encountered Mrs. Wood in the corridor, her arms filled with kindling. "Oh, dear, the furnace is acting up again," she panted, "and Martin's filling up the wood boxes."

"Martin is?" Rae echoed, hardly able to suppress the joy that his name evoked. "Where is he?"

"Let me in your room, dearie, to lay your fire."

"I'll take it," Rae said, reaching for the burden.

"Now, now—likely you'll burn the place down,

dearie. Open the door for me."

"No, Mrs. Wood, I'll attend to it."

The woman's bright eyes turned hard. "You'll do no such thing, Dina! You don't know the first thing about it, and I do, hear? Now unlock that door!"

Rae hesitated. To open the door would reveal the real Dina's presence, while not to do so would arouse the housekeeper's suspicions. "Let me take the kindling," she said more gently, "and you go send Martin up with the logs."

To see him! To confront him with Dina, no matter how much of a shock it might be, and to clear up the mystery for his benefit. It would be a load off her mind and a showdown at last. If he repudiated her for her deception, then so be it! At least she would know.

Mrs. Wood relented reluctantly. Mumbling to herself, she went toward the back stairs. "And I'll take care of things in Grandfather's rooms, too," Rae called after her.

Dina was huddled deep in a chair, a picture of abject misery. The girl seemed always to be cold or wet, Rae thought pityingly. "We'll have you warm in two seconds," she said cheerfully. "Something conked out in the furnace, and Mrs. Wood is sending Martin up with fuel."

Dina rubbed her pale little hands together. "What I want to know is how long I have to stay here like this. I'm getting the heeby-jeebies. I want out!"

Rae waved an arm expansively toward the gathering storm. "Be my guest—go!"

"I didn't mean that, and you know it," Dina sulked.

"And I didn't mean it, either," Rae said with marked restraint. "What I *did* mean is that you're safe and warm, well fed, and you had better count your blessings. How would you like to be back on the sidewalks of the city, wondering where your next meal was coming from?"

"Ugh!"

"Well? Pull your chair closer, and presently I'll bring your supper."

"I'm *bored!*"

"I'll bring you some books and magazines when I get this fire going." *Keep her preoccupied so she won't do something foolish!* "Did you understand what I said—that Martin is coming?"

"So what?"

"So we'll have to explain your presence here—and who I am."

The girl's eyes brightened. "Does that mean that I can—?"

"No, it doesn't. Martin can be trusted, though, to help us if anything happens."

"You mean to Gimpy?"

"To him or any of us. There's an air of tension around here. Mrs. Wood was quite perturbed just now, and I think she's getting suspicious."

"Fat old biddy!"

There was a heavy knock on the door before Rae could reply. She opened it cautiously, her mind whirling with what she must say to Martin. Her spine stiffened. Whatever reaction he showed to the confrontation with the real Dina, *she* must conduct herself with poise and resignation. The time was at hand!

"I—"

He was inside, wood piled high in his enormous arms, and he stood like a great statue, staring at the shivering little figure before the fire.

"Pick!" Rae gathered all her resources to combat the unexpected challenge. "What are you doing here?"

Slowly he wheeled to face her, naked hatred in his eyes as they raked over her features, then swiveled again to Dina. Rae waited, breathless, while Dina returned his gaze contemptuously. Pick hurled the logs into the fireside basket and went down on his knees by the chair.

"Dina, is it you?" he asked humbly.

Her laugh was vitriolic, lashing over him. "Yes, Big Ape! Oh, you fool, you!"

The big man cringed under the sarcasm and mad laughter. Had Rae not been so afraid of him, she would have pitied him. He quivered, his huge hands knotting, his face distorted in purple wrath while the needles of wry mirth pierced him. When he turned to Rae, he said with venom, "I'll get you for this! I'll break that lyin' white neck with my two fists!" He rose to his feet, and Rae crouched against the wall, waiting for the onslaught of those powerful muscles, her eyes closed.

Dina was a dynamo for one so small. She butted her head into his belly and, flailing him with her fists, backed him out of the door. Panting she shot the bolt and whipped around to face Rae.

"Now what do we do?"

CHAPTER FOURTEEN

The battle for survival had begun!

Throughout the long night the two girls clung together, listening to Pick's curses and futile pounding. Mrs. Wood could be heard, too, trying to placate the raging giant, and Greg's voice whining thinly, "What's going on? What's the matter?"

There was a sharp thud, and Rae envisaged Greg's inert body on the floor, struck unconscious by the fury of the maddened foreman. Pick could break the door in, Rae knew, and she hoped his mother's influence would prevail. Stealthily she and Dina moved furniture into place against the door as a barricade.

"He's the one that's insane," Dina whispered. "He's gone completely berserk."

"Never mind that now. Help me with this chest."

"What will Gimpy think?"

"Let's hope that he's asleep and unaware."

Olivia's scream rent the air. "What have you done to my boy? Oh, darling, speak to Mother."

There was a surcease in the attack, and Mrs. Shelby ceased speaking, while a dragging sound replaced the shouting and pounding. "Take him to his room—call the doctor! Oh, the blood!"

"Maybe they'll all kill each other," Dina said mischievously.

"Be quiet!"

"I'm hungr-ry!"

Pick resumed his torture, mumbling now in frustration. There was the sound of something crashing against the heavy door, and splintering.

"Pickeral, Pickeral, that'll do no good! Wait until morning, boy. Let them starve or freeze to death."

"No! I want my Dina!" He began to sob, great racking gasps, breaking down. "Mama, she's in there—laughing at me, while that Jezebel drives her on—"

"Come now, dearie. Remember the Bible? 'An eye for an eye—' "

"I'll poke out her eyes and cut off her fingers, one by one. Oh—"

A sudden silence settled, almost worse than

the noise. Oh, dear, God, where was Martin? Dina moved carefully to the bathroom and brought back two glasses of water. "It helps stave off hunger," she said calmly. "I used to do it all the time after the money ran out and I had nothing to eat."

Rae sipped. She was not hungry, but her stomach was knotted with fear and foreboding. They were at the mercy of a crazed, maddened animal, victims waiting for his return. The fire burned low, and Rae put the last log on it and brought warm robes from the closet for them. Dina sighed long and lustily. "I'm glad you're with me," she said meekly.

"I doubt that you need my protection, you little menace."

"Will he try to get to Gimpy?"

"Not tonight, I think. His main concern is you."

"I wonder what Olivia's thinking."

"About her 'dear boy,' I imagine. Perhaps she's managed to call a doctor by now. Help may be on the way."

"Old Doc Porter?" Dina scoffed. "He's almost as rickety as Grimes and Gimpy."

Rae walked to the window and drew aside the draperies. Snow obscured the waterfall tumbling over the black rocks, but she could hear the force of its gushing. Dim gray light pierced the gloom. What would morning bring? *Where was Martin?*

"Why don't we make a run for Gimpy's room?" Dina asked peevishly. "It might be warmer there."

"Too risky."

"You don't want him to see me, do you?" She began moving away the furniture.

"Now don't get sassy with me, young lady!" Rae warned. "Do you want to be the death of me?"

"Then I'll go and you stay here!" Dina bolted for the door, and they grappled for a moment, Rae hissing dire threats while they struggled. Dina, frail but swift, eluded her grasp and in one quick movement struck away the barricade and darted into the hall and down its dark cavern. Undecided, Rae started to follow but drew back as she heard Pick's bellow. "Gotcha! Aha, what you going to do now? Laugh, Dina— laugh at me!"

"Rae!" Dina screamed.

" 'Rae,' " Pick imitated. "Come out, Rae, and I'll kill you!"

Shivering, Rae withdrew into the room. Could

she be of any help to Dina? No, Pick would not harm the girl he loved. He *would* harm *her*, though, the one to whom he had confessed his misdeeds. In his maddened state he wouldn't hesitate. She felt her body go limp imagining the feeling of those massive hands about her neck, choking the breath from her lungs. There was another embryonic scream from Dina, quickly cut off, and a curse from Pick. He was probably nursing a bite on his hand. Would Mrs. Wood intercede for the girl? Rae sat down to wait developments, her heart pounding with trepidation. Could Pick traverse those rocks under the waterfall as Dina had done? She waited, wondering, as the dull gray dawn slowly crept into the room with chilling fingers.

Dr. Alexander made an unexpected visit two days later.

Rae roused from her torpor as she heard his gutteral voice and the heavy accent. There was another voice, too young and clear, that made her throat clutch with renewed hope. She ran to the door, struggling with the chest and chairs of the barricade, shaking in her haste and calling, "Martin."

She heard his feet on the stairs and, with

one last mighty yank, flung the door open and
ran into his arms.

"Dina—Dina, what the hell's going on here?
Please, darling, stop trembling and tell me!"

Rae reeled away, realizing the danger to him.
"Pick—he's gone mad! Come with me!" Lead-
ing him by the hand, she streaked to Mr. Boulleray's suite and gave the quick raps which were
her and Grimes' signal. Somewhere downstairs
she heard Mrs. Wood remonstrating with the
sturdy doctor.

"Girl dead in the snow—" she said shrilly.
"There's no such thing! The only girl in this
house is upstairs. See here, where do you think
you're going?" This last ended on a cry of
despair. "What did you say?"

"—With his throat cut," the doctor said brok-
enly. "Z-z-z-t! Throat cut, madam!"

"Oh, my God—my boy!" All the anguish of
a mother's heart was in the cry.

Rae urged Martin through the door, her eyes
glazed with horror. Her hand sought his as she
asked through stiff lips: "Is it Dina? Dina and
Pick?"

He pulled her to him, clasping her tightly.
"I thought it was you! Oh, my dear—my very
dear!"

Grimes touched a finger to his lips. "Please, he's asleep. Go in to him, Miss Dina—very quietly, please."

Followed by Dr. Alexander, torn with emotion such as she had never known and choked with tears, Rae went obediently. She took her customary chair by the side of the bed and raised weary eyes to the physician. He patted her shoulder. "Later, he said, not now."

Grimes closed the door on the commotion downstairs, and the only sound in the room was Mr. Boulleray's heavy breathing. Slowly his eyes opened and roved over Rae's face. "You're crying, Deeno! Why?"

She lifted his hand and kissed it. "Because I'm happy, Gimpy."

He smiled wanly at the doctor. "Always when she's happy. Never when she's hurt or mad."

"All right, that's enough emotion," the doctor said practically, his fingers on the old man's pulse. "A thorough examination is—how do you call it?—in order. Yes."

Rae came out into the parlor, her hair disordered and the robe hanging loosely about her. She gestured Grimes into the bedroom and went to Martin, leaning against him weakly. "I never thought he'd hurt her," she cried dismally. "Poor little Dina!"

"He didn't hurt her, dear," he said tenderly "She was running from him, and she tripped— over a root beneath the snow, perhaps—and her neck was broken by the fall. Whatever you're thinking—don't!"

They swayed, clinging to each other in the sharp gray cold.

CHAPTER FIFTEEN

That night at dinner, Dr. Alexander strung the dangling threads together. Rae was rested and relaxed now, with Martin beside her, Grimes caring for the patient upstairs and Letty serving the hearty fare, all unaware of the tragedy.

"I do not pretend to be clairvoyant," the doctor said modestly, "but from the first I sensed something wrong in this house. Dr. Albright, for instance, did not want me on the case."

"But wasn't he the one who brought you here, Doctor?" Rae asked.

Dr. Alexander nodded toward Martin. "Only contrary to his best judgment. Martin, whom I had attended in the hospital, was actually the one who called me."

"You did?" Rae asked of Martin. "Why?"

Martin smiled grimly. "You'll recall that I thought Pick was the one who clouted me."

"Yes."

"And you'll remember what occurred the afternoon that I returned home?"

Rae blushed. They had been in each other's arms when Pick had walked into Martin's room unceremoniously to announce Val's visit. "Yes," she murmured uncomfortably.

He poured cream into his coffee, his voice very low. "When you walked outside with the young man, presumably to dismiss him, Pick began to act very strangely—ranting and raving about your deception, cursing and muttering that you and the Old Man were conspiring to rob him of his rights. It was all so much gibberish to me for a while, if you'll recall, I was considerably confused myself."

Rae flushed even more, and he touched her hand. "I understand now, of course, your trying to extricate yourself from a situation which you found dishonest and distasteful."

"Yes, and I was becoming afraid of Pick. Val —who is married, by the way—was the only person I could think of to appeal to."

"I'm missing the significance of all this," the doctor complained. "How did you discover the man, Pickeral, to be psychotic?"

"Excuse the personal touches, Doctor." Martin chuckled. "There are some things that this girl and I need to clear up. To go on with that afternoon, Pick rushed from the room, very angry, and the next thing I knew, he had attacked Mr. Boulleray and—"

"—And brought on the stroke?" The doctor rubbed his beard thoughtfully. "I see. The patient seems to have no memory of the episode."

"I saw it—saw the result, and called Mrs. Wood."

"Ah! There's an enigma!"

"Mrs. Wood?" Rae said. "Not when you know the circumstances. She, poor woman, is Pick's mother and was completely under his domination." Martin gazed at her speculatively, and she rushed on, "I overheard them talking. It's true!"

"Then that accounts for a great many things," Martin said, "things that puzzled me. When Mr. Boulleray rallied, thanks to this good doctor, Pick retired to re-marshal his forces. I imagine it must have been a sordid revelation to come home and discover *two* Dinas."

"Psychotic," the doctor said. "Dr. Albright knew this and traded upon it. If he could persuade the girl to marry Pick, and Pick could dispose of the Old Man, it would be to his financial advantage. Apparently he sponsored the scheme."

"He must have been somewhat confused by that interview with you, Rae, on the day I was knocked out."

Rae suppressed a smile. "Since I've talked with Dina, I can imagine. He was determined, though, to lay the assault on you at my door. I truly believe now that Pick dissuaded him from taking me back to the Institute."

"Then why did you fear Pick?"

Rae shook her head. "At that time, just intuition, I guess. When I visited you at the hospital, Martin, my fears began to take shape. Then, overhearing that conversation between Pick and Mrs. Wood, I knew that I was right. That was when I started my vigil at Mr. Boulleray's bedside. I felt that I was the only one to protect him and," she added childingly, "you, Martin, had taken a powder."

"Licking my wounds," he said, "and staying away from your vicinity. This morning early, unable to sleep, I was watching the storm from my window over the garage when I saw them."

"Dina and Pick?"

He nodded. "I thought it was you and he, of course, playing in the snow. It hurt that you had turned to him until, all at once, it struck me that neither of you wore any kind of wrap. Dina fell, lying in such a grotesque position that I knew she was hurt badly. I ran to her—your—aid, and found Pick standing over her like a great maddened bear. 'You can't do this to me,' he said. 'You can't escape me this way!' He was about to bring his hands down on her prostrate body when he saw me. He ran off into the forest, and I saw that the girl was dead, her neck broken from the fall. Later they found him with his throat cut."

There was a silence, broken only by Rae's gasp and the sound of the surging waterfall. Letty passed the pantry door with a covered dinner tray for Olivia and Greg. "I'll bring more coffee in a minute," she called.

The doctor rose. "No more for me. I'll look in on my patients and retire for the night. Greg will need a sedative."

Rae caught at his arm. "Do you—have you told Mr. Boulleray yet?"

He smiled down at her indulgently. "Would you destroy this, his most precious possession?"

Rae pondered this for a long moment, her candid gaze never leaving his. "You're asking me to continue this terrible deception? I love him dearly, but I—"

"And he loves you, too, so why not? For the present, at least, the secret is safe with the three of us here, except for Mrs. Wood who is gone and will never, I'm sure, betray the facts. She is too closely involved in all that has happened to reveal herself."

"Won't Olivia and Greg wonder at her sudden departure after so many years?"

The doctor shrugged. "Those two are concerned for themselves alone."

Rae watched him go, sighing deeply as Letty returned with hot coffee. "I seem to be exactly where I was before."

Martin waited until the maid had left before he said, "Not quite. There is a difference now, isn't there?"

"Is there?" she asked roguishly.

"You know it," he replied ardently. "Ah, Rae, darling, if you hadn't come!"

She shook away sudden tears. "Martin, I couldn't be sure that it wasn't Dina, not I, whom you loved. If she had lived—"

"I would have known, darling." He tapped his chest. "Something in here told me all along that this was someone I had never known. Dina was a sweet, pitiful, erratic kid who needed a friend — someone to defend her from Greg's sadism. Too bad I didn't know about Pick, too, before he diverted her mind into dual channels of personality."

"He must have loved her very much," Rae said sadly.

"No more than I love you, Rae, and not so normally." He gestured about the high-ceilinged room. "This place has been host to a conflict of desires long enough, I think. It needs you. *I* need you! Stay, Rae!"

There will be years, she thought, *to wipe away the horror—years to turn this ugly old house into a haven of love!* She leaned across the table, and they framed each other's faces with their hands, blue eyes smiling into brown ones tenderly before their lips met in a sweet and silent pledge. The dark deception was forgotten in a new hope for the future.